THE ARTSY

MISTAKE

MYSTERY

OTHER GREAT MISTAKE MYSTERIES

The Best Mistake Mystery

THE ARTSY MISTAKE MYSTERY

THE GREAT MISTAKE MYSTERIES

sylvia mcnicoll

DUNDURN
TORONTO

Cover image: © Tania Howells
Printer: Webcom

Library and Archives Canada Cataloguing in Publication

McNicoll, Sylvia, 1954-, author
    The artsy mistake mystery / Sylvia McNicoll.

(The great mistake mysteries)
Issued in print and electronic formats.
ISBN 978-1-4597-3880-5 (softcover).--ISBN 978-1-4597-3881-2
(PDF).--ISBN 978-1-4597-3882-9 (EPUB)

    I. Title.

PS8575.N52A89 2017   jC813'.54   C2016-908135-4
                                               C2016-908136-2

1   2   3   4   5   21   20   19   18   17

  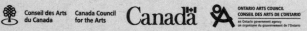

We acknowledge the support of the **Canada Council for the Arts**, which last year invested $153 million to bring the arts to Canadians throughout the country, and the **Ontario Arts Council** for our publishing program. We also acknowledge the financial support of the **Government of Ontario**, through the **Ontario Book Publishing Tax Credit** and the **Ontario Media Development Corporation**, and the **Government of Canada**.

Nous remercions le **Conseil des arts du Canada** de son soutien. L'an dernier, le Conseil a investi 153 millions de dollars pour mettre de l'art dans la vie des Canadiennes et des Canadiens de tout le pays.

Care has been taken to trace the ownership of copyright material used in this book. The author and the publisher welcome any information enabling them to rectify any references or credits in subsequent editions.
                                                                    — *J. Kirk Howard, President*

The publisher is not responsible for websites or their content unless they are owned by the publisher.

Printed and bound in Canada.

VISIT US AT

 dundurn.com | @dundurnpress | 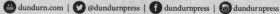 dundurnpress | dundurnpress

Dundurn
3 Church Street, Suite 500
Toronto, Ontario, Canada
M5E 1M2

For anyone who's ever created a masterpiece artwork for the fridge, especially my grands, Hunter, Fletcher, Finley, William, Jadzia, Violet, Desmond, and Scarlett

While the settings and some of the mistakes may be real, the kids, dogs, professors, crossing guards, and neighbours are all made up. If you recognize yourself or anyone else, you've clearly made a mistake. Good for you!

day one

THE GREAT MISTAKE

MYSTERIES

DAY ONE, MISTAKE ONE

Renée and I have an arrangement. In the mornings when I walk my clients Ping and Pong, I swing round to her place and pick her up. She then takes charge of Ping, the hyperactive Jack Russell, a former pound puppy Mrs. Bennett pays me to exercise. I continue with Pong, the taller, quieter greyhound she rescued from Florida.

Renée doesn't like to hang around her house alone, so she doesn't mind leaving way early, the moment her older brother, Attila, takes off for class — he goes to Champlain High. If I were her, I'd want to leave even earlier.

He's scary. His name suits him: Attila, like the Hun. Renée says it's a popular name in Hungary, where her parents were born.

Right now I'm wondering if the arrangement with Renée isn't a mistake. If it is, it'll be the first one I make today, though, and not a big one. It's important to make mistakes, my father tells me all the time. It means we're trying new things, sometimes outside our comfort zone. Being friends with a girl is, for sure, outside my comfort zone, and Renée forces people to pay attention to her. From her se-quined hair barrettes, through to her sparkly glass-es, and all the way down to her light-up sneakers, everything she wears catches your eye. She's also yappy, like Ping, always with one more thing to add or bark about. I'm more like Pong, tall and quiet.

Just not quite as calm.

Both Ping and Pong are white with black mark-ings on the head and a black spot on the body. (Greyhounds aren't always grey. Renée can ex-plain all that to you.) They scramble ahead of me like mismatched horses pulling a carriage: Ping, a scruffy pony; Pong, a smooth-coated stallion.

This morning I can handle them by myself. It's a great fall day, leaves swish as we walk, the sunshine feels warm. Even the hundred-year-old jogger, all bent over at the shoulders and back, wears shorts as he runs past us. The dogs give him a friendly bark of encouragement. Neither makes a lunge for him.

"Good boys!" I tell them.

Today, though, I think the route to Renée's is all wrong for us. Usually, I make the dogs walk to the left of me so that when they go to the bathroom, it's not on someone's lawn. But today is junk pickup day. Once a month the neighbourhood gets to put out any objects, large or small, that they don't want alongside their garbage and recycling, and the city picks them up. Dad calls it redecorating day. He is out walking his five Yorkie clients right now, scouting for a previously enjoyed bookshelf.

This junk slows us down, the large objects attracting the dogs' attention. Sometimes, they bark at them; always, they like to pee on them. First Pong — with his long legs, he trots in the lead — then Ping. Brant Hills Park would be so much better for Ping and Pong's exercise this morning.

"Stop that!" I yank Pong back from someone's recycling bin just as he raises his leg to salute its contents.

Good thing. A banged-up white van pulls up beside us and a dad from our school jumps out to rummage through the recycling.

I want to call out, "Hi, Mr. Jirad." I don't know his son, Reuven, super well, but I helped deliver his paper route last week with Renée. Mr. Jirad concentrates on pulling out liquor bottles from the box and doesn't notice us.

Maybe this is embarrassing for him. I'm going to pretend I don't notice him, either, then. As he drives away, I see the big dent in the back of his van all caulked in with some kind of filler. A home repair that doesn't quite work. Over the painted filler, wobbly black letters spell *Pay the artist*.

"I didn't know Mr. Jirad was an artist," I tell the dogs.

Ping growls, eyes intent on a teenager in a black hoodie and bright, flowered leggings. The sunlight glints off the diamond stud in her nose as she pulls the ugliest wall plaque I've ever seen from someone's pile of junk. It's a large grey fish, mouth open, pointy teeth drawn, mounted on a flat slab of glossy wood. Maybe Ping is growling at the fish, not the girl. In any case, I strain to hold on to both dogs.

She smiles as she admires the fish.

"It looks real," I can't help commenting as we get closer to the pile. The fish is bent as though it's wriggling in a stream.

"It *is* real! Taxidermy."

I wince. "And you like it?"

"It's perfect!" She looks from the fish to me. "Oh, not for me. The plaque is for my prof. They're redecorating the staff lounge."

"Perfect," I repeat, wondering about her professor.

She nods and grins as she walks away with her prize.

"Good dogs," I tell Ping and Pong as we continue on. So far so good, anyway. Although, it's not just the busyness of the route to Renée's house that makes me wonder if our arrangement is a mistake. Does she expect me to share the money I've earned? I officially work for Dad's company, Noble Dog Walking. Noble is our last name.

Also, if she wasn't hanging around me so much, would I have a chance to make a real friend? Like Jessie. We used to have sleepovers in his pool house before he moved away last summer. Dad's never going to let me bunk in the same room as a girl.

Ping and Pong pull hard now, Ping wagging his stub of tail like crazy.

A couple houses ahead, I see Mrs. Whittingham loading up all the children in her shiny black van. She operates a home daycare and it seems like she stuffs about ten kids in that van. She slides the door closed and then gives a friendly honk as she drives past us. The kids point and wave at the dogs. The dogs wag back.

That distracts me for a minute, and when Pong yanks toward the house near us, toward Mr. Rupert's wishing well, I nearly miss what he's up to.

"Oh, no you don't! Your wishes won't come true that way." I pull him back. Mr. Rupert is the neighbourhood grouch and he got scary mad when Pong went number two in his flower bed last walk, even though I was cleaning it up before he started yelling.

Ping doesn't like me scolding Pong and starts barking, sharp and loud. Ping, even though he's a quarter of Pong's size, likes to defend Pong when he's not fighting with him himself.

"Don't worry, I'm not mad at Pong."

Apparently defending his bigger pal is not what Ping is up to today because he's not looking my way. Instead, he strains at his leash toward Mrs. Whittingham's house on the corner. When I don't move quickly enough toward it, he bounces up and down on his hind legs like they're bedsprings.

"What's up, boy?" I ask. "Do you see something?" He can get excited about the slightest thing. A small black bag of dog doo sitting in a tree set him off a week ago. I thought that was kind of weird, myself. As we draw closer to Mrs. Whittingham's house, Pong pulls, too, and I see what they want to investigate.

From the tree in Mrs. Whittingham's yard, a yellow plastic swing moves slightly in the breeze.

It looks like there's something sitting in it, too big for a bird or squirrel, bigger than a raccoon … oh, no … she's left a kid behind in the swing!

The little boy looks paper white with purple circles under his eyes … like he's, like he's … but he can't be; she only left a minute ago.

I run with the dogs to her house, dash up her lawn, bashing my knee on some stupid bird ornament. *Ow.* Then I grab for the boy in the swing. I think I've seen enough rescue videos that I can use CPR to bring him back to life if I have to.

That is … if it's not too late.

"Hey, you! What the heck are you doing!" A voice blasts from behind me.

"What …"

"I know it's butt ugly, but you leave that Halloween display just the way you found it."

Okay, this is definitely mistake number one of the day, and it's a doozy. Mr. Rupert catches me rescuing some kind of creepy lifelike doll.

DAY ONE, MISTAKE TWO

Halloween display? Mrs. Whittingham must have just set it up — early bird of the neighbourhood — no one else has so much as a black cat up. I drop the corpse-like doll back in its seat.

Mr. Rupert's face wrinkles into a full frown reaching from his eyebrows down to his chin. His yellow hair sticks up like short lightning bolts. He folds his arms across his chest and squints at me. "Were you the one who stole my mailbox?"

"No, no! Of course not."

He has a "Support Our Troops" sticker on his car's bumper, a bright green Cadillac, and Renée swears she saw him in camouflage combat fatigues last Sunday. Even by the way he stands — back straight, legs apart — you know he's a military man. Who would be crazy enough to take anything from him?

"Then why are you trespassing on private property?" he shouts in a cannon-shot voice.

"I thought the baby was real." As I stop to look around now, I realize the bird ornament I knocked

over is a large black plastic raven with blood painted down its beak. Styrofoam grave markers zigzag
in a straggly pattern across the lawn. They have
cutesy sayings: "Here rests Eddie, he died in beddy."
Pong is peeing on that tombstone right now.

I'm usually so much more observant than this.

Mr. Rupert shakes his head. "What exactly do
you take me for?"

A grump. Not like I'm going to tell him that. I
heard he's a gun collector. Instead I try to explain.
"Well, Mrs. Whittingham just drove off. I thought
maybe with all those kids, she may have left one
behind." What I didn't say is that she has been
known to make crazy mistakes, too. She locked
the keys and a couple of the littler kids in the car
one day, and I let her use my cellphone to call the
cops. Her phone was locked in the car with the
kids. She was so embarrassed. I know how that
feels, so I never told anyone.

Still, would she leave a child in a swing? I move
the dogs out of the way and straighten up the raven.

"That's better!" Mr. Rupert calls. "Now I'm going
to check my surveillance camera. I better not catch
you on it."

Surveillance camera, gah! As I said, last week I
helped Renée deliver newspapers for Reuven, the
kid in the house next door to her. Mr. Rupert gets
the paper. Of course I'm going to be on that camera.

"My wife made that mailbox," Mr. Rupert continues, staring into my eyes, "and you better believe I'll find out who stole it." His eyes are large, anime-sized blobs of dark brown quicksand. He tries to drown me with his stare.

I blink first.

Then he jabs his finger in Ping and Pong's direction. "Don't let me catch those animals defecating on my lawn."

"No, sir!"

"On your way!" He points and watches as we move toward the sidewalk. Then he marches back into the house.

Phew! My heart keeps pounding double time.

The dogs and I turn the corner to Renée's house. Up the walkway, the dogs crowd together in front of me as I reach to ring the doorbell.

Renée answers before I finish ringing. She's wearing a pink sweater with a rainbow-striped vest and red pants. Flashy and clashy all at the same time. "You're two minutes late. Step in for a moment while I get my things."

If I'm two minutes late, why doesn't she have her stuff together already?

In the small foyer, Ping sniffs around a large duffle bag. "Stop that." I pull him back. While I focus on him, Pong nuzzles into the bag and pulls out a wooden shape. Before I can snatch it out from his long snout, he slumps down and gnaws at it.

Renée comes back in that moment. "Oh, no! Don't let him chew Attila's fish!"

"Well, I didn't *let* him …" We both kneel down to wrestle his new wooden chew toy away from him. "I thought Attila was finished his community service!"

"No. He has to cut out the wooden fish for *all* the schools signed up for Stream of Dreams, not just Brant Hills. These are for Bruce T. Lindley."

I pinch the corners of Pong's mouth between my thumb and pointer finger and press gently. "Oh, man. He complained enough when he delivered ours."

"Yeah." Renée scrunches her mouth. "Well, it *was* tons of work for him." Renée tugs at the wooden shark shape. Ping barks. "Got it," Renée says. "Sit, Ping, quiet!" She raises her finger at the little dog and instantly he drops his haunches, waiting for a treat. Renée holds up the rescued hammerhead shark. "Oh, great, there are teeth marks on this one."

"It's a shark that's been in a battle. Stuff it back in the bag." I hold it open for her. "Attila probably made extra."

"This is his last batch. He should be in a better mood after this."

"Wasn't he a little happy to do something for the environment?" I reach into my pocket and give Ping and Pong each one of Dad's legendary homemade liver bites. The fish were a lot of fun for us. Not so much knowing that real fish are poisoned by garbage dumped in the stream — which is why the project started — but painting the wooden models.

Renée nods. "Except Attila complained that the tank he spray-painted on Champlain High's wall had an important environmental message, too."

"It was a nice tank. I loved the 3D effect; it looked like it was crashing out of the school." Definitely was a bit scary, too, though I don't tell her that.

"Your whale is terrific, too," Renée said. "A Green Lantern whale, so creative."

"Green and white are my favourite colours." Green Lantern is also my nickname at school 'cause Bruno and Tyson saw my superhero boxers once when I changed for gym back in grade four.

Renée stares at the duffle bag. "I wonder why the fish are still here. The Bruce T. Lindley kids are done the environmental part of the project. They're supposed to paint these today."

"Maybe Attila forgot to deliver them." I smile. A big mistake on Attila's part.

Renée sighs. "Imagine all the kindergarteners standing around in their smocks with nothing to paint."

It's comforting to know that even tough Attila can forget something as important as this. The idea makes me feel generous. "I know, why don't we bring them to the school for him?"

"Are you sure? It's a fifteen-minute walk between Bruce T. and Brant Hills. We'll have to take Ping and Pong with us or we'll be late."

"Absolutely." Brant Hills is where we go to school, grade seven. Bruce T. Lindley only goes to grade six. I pick up the duffle bag, then drop it again on my feet.

Ow, ow, ow! My second mistake of the day. I've raised Renée's hopes — now I'm going to have to let her down. "These fish weigh a ton. There's no way I can carry them all the way to Bruce T."

DAY ONE, MISTAKE THREE

Compared to Attila forgetting the wooden fish blanks in the first place, trying to lift them all at once is a just a weensy error in judgment. Attila is bigger and pumps iron, so he can probably do it with one hand.

Renée crumples her eyebrows. "Attila will get in so much trouble if the school doesn't get these this morning."

"Well, then, maybe we can divide them up."

"Okay, except … there's another bag in the hall. Let me check. OMG, yes, this one is full of fish, too." Renée drags a second, larger hockey bag from the other end of the hall.

"No way." I shake my head. "Okay, wait, maybe …
what about a wagon? Do you have one?"

"No." Renée snaps her fingers. "But Reuven does."

"Right, that red metal number. The one we used
to deliver the *Post*."

"He'll let us borrow it for sure."

"All right then!"

Ping yips his excitement.

Stepping around Ping and Pong, we drag the
bags to the front door. Then Renée runs to ring
Reuven's doorbell while I hold on to the dogs.

No answer, but I see his wagon at the side of the
house. Just sitting there, waiting. Ping ruffs and
Pong raises one tall ear when Renée rings the bell a
second time.

"We're going to be late," I call to her.

She nods, looks around hopefully, then just
grabs the wagon. "We'll return it before he even notices it's gone. He won't mind." She races it back to
the front of her house.

"Does he have a surveillance camera?" I ask as
she approaches.

"I don't think so. Why?"

"'Cause Mr. Rupert has one and his mailbox
got stolen." In my mind, I can picture Mr. Rupert
dressed in a camouflage uniform, stalking someone
with a rifle in his arms. I turn to look at Renée's
face. "You don't think Attila took it, do you?"

"Not his style. Now, if someone had spray-painted a war scene on his walls, I would be suspicious …"

"Mr. Rupert would probably like a war scene on his walls."

"You've got a point, there." Renée lifts one end of the hockey bag and I the other, in order to hoist it on to the wagon. The bag completely fills it. Then I sit the duffle bag on top. The sides are really low on this wagon, not like those tall plastic ones with built-in comfy seats for kids. Still, there's no way we're making two trips.

We start to walk slowly, the duffle bag shifting with every crack and bump in the sidewalk. Holding Pong's leash makes it even more awkward to pull the overloaded wagon.

"I can take a turn with the wagon," Renée offers. I give her the handle. But it becomes trickier when Ping dives to nip at the wheels.

"Here, give it back." Now I have a genius idea. I wind Pong's leash through the handle and, still gripping the loop of it, allow Pong to do most of the pulling. Ping keeps nipping at the wheels, and it's hard steering him and the wagon. But the school is only a block away. We should make it in plenty of time.

As Pong tugs the wagon around the corner back the way we came, near Mrs. Whittingham's house,

I tell Renée about her amazing Halloween display. "Wait till you see the doll in the swing. It's so lifelike that …" My mouth drops open.

The yellow swing moves gently in the breeze, empty now.

"Guess she took it in," Renée suggests. "Maybe it scared the little kids."

"Her van isn't back yet, though." I try to look through the windows but the curtains are closed. "Her raven and tombstones are missing, too."

"Early for Halloween, anyway," Renée says.

"I just hope Mr. Rupert doesn't blame me." But I know he will. He saw me lifting that doll. And just like he will never let me forget that Pong pooped on his flowers, he won't let this go, either.

"Why would he think you did this?"

"Because …" I don't really want to explain, and at that moment, Ping starts growling, a rumbling, low big-dog kind of growl. Surprising from such a pipsqueak spring coil, really.

A woman in a bulky blue coat with an orange vest overtop approaches. She's wearing dark sunglasses and a police-type cap. Her face is vampire white and her hair hangs down as flat and straight as a crow's wings. At her side she carries a stop sign. Our new crossing guard — Madame X the kids call her because there's a yellow X of reflective tape across the back of her orange safety vest.

The stop sign may be upsetting Ping. He doesn't like buses, skateboards, people in hoodies or with packages and umbrellas, and now, I guess, women in bulky coats with stop signs.

Closer and closer she comes. I can't tell if she notices us or not because of her sunglasses.

Ping's rumbly growl sets Pong off. Suddenly, he jerks the wagon forward. The top bag of fish pitches to the side. I make a grab for it a second too late. The bag tumbles. Wooden fish blanks clatter everywhere.

Madame X raises her stop sign high. When it comes down, it will slice Pong right through. Ping barks hysterically.

Renée throws her arms out to protect the dog.

But Madame X drops to her knees, placing the sign down next to her. "Dare, dare, nice doggy." She reaches out with her black-gloved fingers and pats Ping.

Ping drops even lower.

"I can geeve heem treat, yes?" She asks me, probably because I'm wearing my uniform, complete with our Noble Dog Walking paw print logo across the shirt pocket.

"Um, sure."

"I'm meesing my own Jack Russell from when I was leetle girl." She gives him a small milk bone. "Cheese flavour," she tells him and then holds a bigger one out for Pong. "Bacon."

Ping flips to his back and she strokes his belly.

Meanwhile, I stuff all the fish back into the bag.

"Eez good you took down those ugly feesh. They block my view and I can't see dee keedies when I'm doing crossing."

Mistake number three of the day goes to Madame X for thinking these wooden blanks are actually the painted ones used to decorate the fence around our kindergarten play area. Yes, I think it's fair to count adults' mistakes, too. They're always quick to point out kids' mistakes, after all.

I open my mouth to tell her these are fish blanks, not the painted ones from our school fence. At that moment a few notes of Beethoven's Fifth plays from Renée's backpack.

She removes her cell from a side pocket and checks the screen. "It's Attila." She frowns as she reads. "He's panicking. He borrowed one of the shop cars to deliver the fish, but when he came home, they were gone."

Well, okay then, check Madame X's whoopsie. We clearly made the bigger mistake; let's call ours mistake number three of the day. Struggling to do moody Attila a favour 'cause we thought he forgot his community commitment, we underestimated him. Attila just figured out an easier way.

DAY ONE, MISTAKE FOUR

Madame X continues walking toward Brant Hills, while Renée and the dogs and I scuttle awkwardly in the other direction toward Bruce T. Lindley's parking lot to meet Attila.

He's waiting for us by the time we get there. Tall, with a black, pointy mohawk and heavy gorilla arms, he gives no wave or hello, just a grunt: "Give me those." He grabs the handle and drags the wagon toward the front door.

"We need to return Reuven's wagon," Renée calls brightly as we follow behind. She's one-third his size and acts three times as cheerful.

"Wait out here! They" — Attila points down at the dogs — "can't come in."

As he pulls the wagon up the front steps, *bump, bump, bump*, the duffle bag tips and spills again. Attila curses, and as he collects the fish, mutters something that sounds like, *"Hate, hate, hate."*

We scramble to help him, I don't know why. When we're finished, he grumbles, "Stupid fish."

Then he disappears into the school for what seems like hours.

"Hope they don't notice the teeth marks on the shark," Renée says.

"The kid that gets it will," I answer. "But maybe they'll like the teeth marks."

Finally, Attila comes back outside, returning Reuven's empty wagon to us. He grumbles again, nothing that sounds like a thank you, then drives off in the old, yellow Saturn they've been working on in shop class.

I can't help shaking my head. "Well, that was pleasant."

Renée frowns. "Attila's got a lot on his mind."

"What? Did he get a new video game?" I can never understand why Renée sticks up for Attila. He's not very nice to her.

"No! He has a deadline to apply for Mohawk College. Or Dad says he'll send him to military college. And he needs a portfolio."

"Uh-huh." We start back to Reuven's house with the wagon and dogs. "You know, his art *is* brilliant. Too bad it's always spray-painted on a wall."

"Yeah, well so is Banksy's." Renée told me about Banksy before. He's a British street artist famous for his graffiti and, yes, it's very cool. But the art seems a bit angry, too. Just like Attila.

"Bet Banksy never got into a college with it."

"So you get Attila's problem. Having to jig saw those fish pieces for the Stream of Dreams projects took all of his spare time, too."

Actually, I understand her family's problem. Renée tells me her parents always fight about

Attila. While their dad wants to send him away, his mom thinks he's gifted and misunderstood.

Gifted and grumpy, I think.

As we get to Reuven's house, I check the outside for surveillance cameras. None. Good. We park the wagon. Then we jog with the dogs down a paved shortcut. They gallop ahead, loving the extra action.

The shortcut continues through three streets and lands us across the road from our school, Brant Hills.

There, Madame X waves her stop sign at cars to help some little kids and their mom get to the other side. And that's when I realize something's wrong.

The mom takes the kids in through the kinder-garten play area and I watch as they start playing on some trikes behind the wire fence.

"Hey," I tell Renée, "I can see the kindergarteners."

"You're right. Oh my gosh. The fish are missing from the fence!"

"I em so happy you took dem down," Madame X says as she walks us to the other side. She points to the play area. "Look at those cute keedies." She smiles as a little boy waves a mini hockey stick at a girl on a trike.

"But the fish were colourful and happy looking," Renée says. "Art-ee-fish-ful," Madame X says. She blows into her whistle sharply. "Leetle boy, stop that! You don't heet people with hockey stick."

He doesn't listen to Madame X, but the duty

teacher hears her and breaks the two kids up.

Renée and I don't have time to investigate the missing fish right now. We need to get Ping and Pong home, and I still want to change out of my Noble Dog Walking uniform before we go to school.

More recycling bins and a mattress and a sofa slow us down as the dogs continue to investigate everything on the way back toward the Bennetts' house.

At one curbside, a plastic toy kitchen set with a stove and fridge and cupboards stops me. "*Aww*. I used to have one of these!" I turn the knobs on the stove just because, and the little round elements turn red. "No!" I push Pong away when he lifts up his long back leg.

We keep walking. The hundred-year-old jogger passes us, just barely. The dogs bark. Renée calls, "Good morning."

He touches his cap. We hang back to give him time to clear some distance.

"I don't get it," Renée says. "Why does he wear that jacket with his jogging shorts?"

"To carry his pacemaker?" I suggest.

"Oh, he's not that old. He's just scrunched up from working at his desk."

"How do you know?" I'm not sure why I even ask. Renée always knows everything.

"My mom hired him to coach Attila — you know — on his portfolio. Mr. Kowalski used to be head of the art department at Mohawk." We start walking and close in on a new pile of junk. Renée stops. "Aw, look, someone's throwing out a picture!"

Leaning against the garbage can is a framed painting of a boy and a rabbit in the snow near a farm. "That's too bad. I kind of like it," I say. But there's no time for me to rescue it and make it to school on time.

The recycling truck lumbers up alongside us now, and both dogs go crazy. The driver dumps some newspapers and clankity bottles into the back of it, then some cardboard tied together with white string.

Rouf, rouf, rouf!

No artwork, kitchen sets, or mattresses — that's for a separate pickup. The driver hops back in the cab and throws a lever.

Ping's barking takes on a new frantic pitch as the truck starts to shuffle from side to side, in kind of a Watusi. It's like the driver has turned on the vehicle's digestive system and the truck needs to shake down all the food.

Mistake number four turns out to be watching the strange dance. We should have been watching our dog clients at all times, keeping them safe and out of mischief.

DAY ONE, MISTAKE FIVE

When the truck finally moves on again, the dogs turn super quiet. Good. We're really close to their house now. Tails stop wagging. Ping and Pong know the fun is over. At the Bennetts' bungalow, I pull the key from one of my pockets, unlock the door, and unleash them.

They slump down at either end of the white-tiled hall, quiet. That's not like Ping at all.

"He's got something in his mouth," Renée says.

Ping's eyes shift around guiltily as I drop to my knees to check.

"Where did he get this?" I gently pry a painted bass from his mouth. The bass has messy green scales and sad black blobs for eyes.

"Pong has one, too." Renée holds up a swordfish.

"That looks like Bruno's Stream of Dreams creation. See the blob of white near the sword part?"

"And the bass belongs to Tyson. They both picked the biggest fish and then did sloppy paint jobs." Renée shakes her head.

"I didn't see where the dogs picked them up, did you?"

"Nuh-uh."

"Too bad. Could be our Stream of Dreams thief." Both of us think on this, first quietly, then outside our heads. "Has to be from one of the junk piles," I say.

"Really? Who would dump stolen art right in front of their house?" Renée asks. "Kind of bold. Isn't that just asking to be caught?"

"True. Besides which, if someone stole them, why would they just chuck them?"

"Well, Madame X wanted them off the fence," Renée insists. "No one else seems to be upset about them disappearing, either." We look at each other.

I can't obsess about this too long. Mom tells me that never helps. I must move on. The dogs stand around me, watching, big-eyed with attention. They want their chew toys back. I don't know what to do with the paint-blobbed fish, but I sure don't want Ping and Pong to get splinters in their mouths. "Oh well," I finally say and shove the fish in one of the bigger pockets on my pants.

"Better fill up their water," I tell Renée. A delay tactic. I always feel bad leaving them. Renée gives Pong pats and Ping flips over for rubs.

"Gotta go, guys," I tell them, giving Ping's belly a last rub. Then Renée and I leave quickly. It's like ripping off a bandage.

As I lock the door behind us, I can hear Ping's yap of disappointment.

Renée shrugs her shoulders at me. Hardest part of dog walking. Worse than scooping poop, even.

Next we stop at my house so I can change out of my Noble Dog Walking shirt. I keep the cargo pants of the uniform on. I grab my lunch from the counter. It's in a plastic box with sections to keep the apple wedges and carrot sticks from touching my cream cheese sandwich. No accidentally grabbing a bag full of defrosting blood-dripping liver today. I did that last week when I left my backpack at school and Dad put my sandwich in a plastic grocery bag. We learn from our mistakes, I think happily. I don't forget my backpack, either; my agenda's been signed. My teacher, Mrs. Worsley, is big on that. Even if there's no homework, Mom or Dad have to initial that they know this.

"Want a granola bar?" I ask Renée as I grab one for on the way.

"Okay."

I pitch it to her. We walk to school together, chewing on chocolate-covered oatmeal bars. We're going to be on time. I feel good. It's a pretty ordinary day so far. There's going to be a perfectly logical explanation for the fish disappearing, I know it. A missing mailbox, a stolen Halloween display, no biggie. I know if Mom were around and not on layover in Amsterdam, she'd say none of those are my problems, anyway.

We arrive at school just in time for the second bell, so no late slip needed. As always, we start the day singing the national anthem and then listening to morning announcements. Our principal,

Mrs. Watier, says nothing about the Stream of Dreams fish disappearing from the fence. You would think she might explain if it was some kind of routine fish cleaning or relocating project, but then, my parents tell me I overanalyze things, so I try to put it out of my mind. One of the grade eight girls begins reading our morning inspiration, but in the middle of it, she stops. We hear some mumbling in the background and then Mrs. Watier interrupts:

"Your attention, please. Everyone stop what you are doing and listen. This is a lockdown. I repeat: we are in lockdown. Please proceed to a lockdown position."

"Why?" I want to scream, but instead, I take a deep breath. And then another. Maybe those breaths sound loud against the sudden silence. Maybe the blood is draining from my face because my head feels swirly.

Tyson rolls his eyes and punches me. "Calm down, Green Lantern. It's just a drill."

But Mrs. Worsley immediately shuts our door and locks it. In a pinched, quiet voice, she speaks. "Grade seven, this is very important. We are now going to do everything exactly as we practised a few weeks ago, do you remember? Everyone, into our safe corner."

Does this have anything to do with the missing fish? Not unless the disappearance is linked to some kind of gunman loose in the school. Oh my gosh,

Mr. Rupert! Did he review the surveillance video and come looking for me? I take another breath. I am not going to panic like I did for the fire alarm last week. That turned out to be a bomb scare. Together with everyone else in the class, I hurry to huddle in our safe corner.

Outside, I see the sun shining and a police car pulling into the parking lot. For a lockdown drill, the police come, so this does not have to mean disaster. I'm not going to leap up and yell at everyone to hide. In fact, I kneel down calmly beside Renée. Tyson must be right after all. This has to be a drill.

Mrs. Worsley's roll of tape squeals as she sticks chart paper over the window in our door.

A second and then a third squad car pull in behind the first one.

That doesn't happen in a drill. Mistake number five has to be thinking any thought that ever comes out of Tyson's mouth is right.

DAY ONE. MISTAKE SIX

I keep breathing deeply so the drum in my chest stops beating as hard. But as Mrs. Worsley pulls the string to close the blinds, they clatter down loudly and I jump. So does Renée. We knock into each other.

Mrs. Worsley puts her finger to her lips and waves our group closer together. Standing in front of us, Mrs. Worsley folds her arms across her chest. She's shorter than I am but fierce, like an eagle. She makes me feel safe.

Renée sits next to me on the floor. Staying quiet is a really impossible job for her. Behind her red glasses, her eyes pop. I can smell brown sugar and wonder if that is coming from her skin — some kind of bath lotion or cream — or whether I am going to have a seizure. I read about people smelling strange things before having one; usually, it's burnt toast, though. The rest of the class shuffles around. The floor feels harder than usual against my butt, so I shift myself, too, but can't find a comfortable position.

Mrs. Worsley looks at us, and with her finger, counts us, mouthing the numbers. She nods as she finishes and smiles. Then she picks up our read-aloud book, *The Night Gardener*, and begins to whisper from it. It's a scary story about a spooky tree that grows in a mansion and manages to control everyone who lives in it. Mrs. Worsley whispering the story is making it scarier today, but in a good way. That tree can't hurt us, after all, and what- or whoever is causing this lockdown seems another world away as I listen.

Even though I called her *Mom* once accidentally at the beginning of the year, and that was a pretty embarrassing mistake, worst of that day, I realize I have never liked Mrs. Worsley more than I do right now.

She reads two entire chapters. When the intercom turns on again and Mrs. Watier announces the lockdown is over, I am hooked on the story and disappointed we can't continue. I must check out Brant Hills library and see if they have the book. I need to know what happens next.

Mrs. Watier explains that the police have searched the entire school and have assured her that there is no danger to any of the staff or students. But she doesn't explain what caused her to call a lockdown and she doesn't say anything about the missing fish.

Mrs. Worsley asks Renée and me to open the blinds again, and it's still a sunny October morning out there. Nothing has changed. No bodies, no fires or bomb squad. But also no fish on the fence.

She asks Tyson to take down the chart paper.

We continue on with math as though nothing happened. Mrs. Worsley talks to us about estimating and rounding a number to the nearest ten to make it easier to add or subtract. She shows us a problem on the Smart Board. "Bronte Creek holds a nest of fish eggs and this nest contains 544 eggs. If 322 hatch, how many did not hatch?"

The problem makes me think of our missing painted fish. If there are 250 students at Brant Hills, there has to have been that many fish on the fence. They were each attached with two heavy metal staples; it would have taken a long time to remove them. Someone should have seen it.

"Stephen?"

"Yes, Mrs. Worsley."

"How many fish?"

I'm confused for a moment. How does she know I'm thinking about those missing Stream of Dreams fish?

"Two hundred and twenty-two!" Renée calls out.

Now here's where Jessie would have been a way better friend. He would never have shown me up like that. Even if a teacher called on him after me, he'd pretend not to know the answer. Probably, he wouldn't even have had to pretend. Renée is just not great at being quietly smart.

"Raise your hand and wait till you're called on, Renée." Mrs. Worsley knits her woolly eyebrows together. "Class? Is she right?"

Renée's always right but I'm not going to answer.

"Remember, we're estimating." Her mouth purls. "We round to the nearest ten. For that, we round 544 down to 540 and drop the two from 322 to make it 320. Now, we subtract 320 from 540. The answer is approximately two hundred and twenty."

"But it's easy to subtract 322 from 544 and get the exact figure," Renée says.

She can't help herself. She doesn't mean to argue, but it sure comes across that way.

Mrs. Worsley closes her eyes for just a moment, then opens them again. "But we wouldn't be estimating, would we, Renée? In estimating, we round off the numbers to the nearest tens."

"But who would want to round off a number when they could have the exact one?"

Plenty of people, I think. Me, for example. It's not like we're measuring the fish for suits or anything. Now, if we needed one wooden fish per student, I would count out the students in each classroom exactly. Or round up. Hopefully, they rounded up so no one has to paint the fish the dogs chewed.

"Excuse the interruption, but would Stephen Noble and Renée Kobai come to the office, please? Stephen Noble and Renée Kobai."

I look around in a panic. The other kids stare at us. This can only mean one thing.

Police questioning! They're going to put us in a room with double-sided mirrors that they can see through to watch us.

Renée grabs my hand as she stands up, forcing me to my feet, too. I quickly shake myself loose. Then she leads the way out the door to the office.

I can see him through the window. It's that police officer with the dog, Troy.

He opens the door for us and Renée immediately calls out: "I remember you. You're the police officer who blew up Reuven's science project!"

Renée's right about the policeman waiting for us in the principal's office. He searched the school with Troy during the bomb scare. With his black muzzle and blond fur, I'd know that golden shepherd anywhere, and he knows us. He's wagging his tail.

After Troy sniffed out Reuven's backpack in the computer lab, the remote-control robot removed it to X-ray it. When it showed the wires of his homemade radio science project, the robot took it to the sandbox and exploded it.

But did Renée have to remind the officer about his mistake? Couldn't she have just said she remembered him from the roof or something? That's where we first met him and Troy; they were searching from the top of the school down. Renée doesn't exactly put the police officer in a good mood.

"I am Constable Jurgensen." He thumbs back toward a woman with a French braid tucked into her police cap. "And this is Constable Wilson. You are the kids with the greyhound and the Jack Russell terrier. Renée and Stephen, am I right?"

We nod.

"Sit down. We want to ask you some questions." Constable Jurgensen doesn't sound friendly and even Troy stops wagging at us. That's Renée's mistake, number six of the day. Reminding the constable about something that puts him in a very bad mood.

DAY ONE, MISTAKE SEVEN

"Ask away." I smile just a little to show the officers we're friendly and co-operative. But not so much that they think we're laughing at them. Renée and I each take a chair. "We'd be happy to answer anything we can."

"Good," Constable Wilson says, smiling. "That's great."

Troy's muzzle opens into a happy pant. It looks as though he's grinning at us.

"Did either of you see anybody suspicious around the school this morning when you were walking the dogs?" Constable Jurgensen asks, one eyebrow at attention.

"Hmm, no, we arrived at school a little later than usual," Renée says.

"That's right, we headed toward Bruce T. Lindley first," I add.

Troy wags as though he likes our answers.

"So you didn't see anyone enter the school armed with a gun?" Constable Jurgensen continues.

I gasp. *Oh, no, Mr. Rupert!* I shake my head.

"No, sir," Renée answers.

"What about last night?" Constable Wilson asks. If they're playing good cop, bad cop, I think she's the nice one. I notice she's the one who holds Troy's leash. "Or early this morning?"

I shake my head.

"Did you notice anybody different hanging around? Any unusual activity?" Constable Jurgensen barks. Troy woofs, too.

Constable Wilson loosens her hold on Troy.

"Nothing," I say.

Constable Jurgensen's nose and eyes seem to sharpen. "You sure? You live close by, don't you?"

"I do." I point to Renée. "She doesn't."

Troy steps forward, sniffing my pant leg.

I shuffle uncomfortably.

"You don't look so good." Constable Jurgensen's voice turns hard. "You feeling guilty over stealing the Stream of Dreams display from the fence?"

"No!" I squeak. I can almost hear the fish in my pocket clack together as I jump.

Troy woofs again.

"We didn't steal the display," Renée says. "Why would we?"

Constable Wilson clears her throat. "The crossing guard, Mrs. Filipowicz, says she saw you with wooden fish in your wagon."

Troy sniffs a little higher on my pant leg.

"Those weren't fish from the school's kindergarten fence. They belonged to my brother, Attila."

"Attila!" Constable Jurgensen exclaims. Then he turns to Constable Wilson and explains, "He's the juvenile who spray-painted the high school."

"Yes, but he's paid his debt to society," Renée says. "He made the fish blanks for the Stream of Dreams project for both schools."

I jump in. "Madame X, um, Mrs. Filipowicz, saw us taking the blanks to Bruce T. Lindley."

Constable Wilson squints at us. "Attila didn't come into this building, did he?"

"No! He goes to Champlain High not Brant Hills."

Will Renée tell them that Attila borrowed a shop car to deliver the blanks to Bruce T.? Did he have permission from the shop teacher? Or would using the Saturn be considered theft, too?

For once, Renée stays quiet. I think she does the right thing.

"So you don't know anything about the disappearance of the fish from the fence?" Constable Jurgensen asks.

I should tell the police about those wooden fish in my pocket right now. But they'll think we're involved, for sure, when we don't know a thing. I stick my hand on top of them. The bass and swordfish feel as if they have come alive and want to leap out of my pocket.

Troy seems to sense this and jumps up.

"What do you have in your pocket?" Constable Wilson asks.

"Liver bites," I answer, pulling a zip-lock bag from the other side. "My dad makes them. Can I give Troy one?"

"Absolutely not," Constable Jurgensen says.

Troy keeps his paws on my legs and wags his tail.

"Sorry, boy," I say, and scratch behind his ears.

"Do you mind showing us what you have in your other pocket?" Constable Wilson asks.

My face heats up like tomato soup. Now what?

I knew I should have pulled out the swordfish and bass the moment Constable Jurgensen mentioned the Stream of Dreams project. Before even. The moment we walked into the office, I should have asked why the fish had disappeared from the fence and shown the police the two that the dogs picked up somewhere along our walk.

Instead, slowly, reluctantly, I remove the painted bass and swordfish from my pocket now.

Renée jumps in quickly. "Ping and Pong had those in their mouths when we took them home. We have no idea where they came from." She talks so fast, even I think she's guilty. Troy whines and slumps down.

"Really?" Constable Jurgensen says. "You sure they didn't pick them up from Attila's room?"

"What?" I squawk. "We weren't even in Renée's house. Well, we were, but just for a moment in the front hall."

"So did the dogs pick them up in the front hall?" Constable Wilson asks.

"No!"

"You said you had no idea where the dogs found the painted fish. Now, you're sure they didn't get them from Attila."

"Because that's where we found the blanks that we delivered to Bruce T. Lindley," Renée explains. "The dogs stole blank fish from the bag in the hall."

"I think they picked the painted ones from some recycling bin on Duncaster," I tell them. "They may have even fallen off the truck."

"Do you know if your brother owns a gun?" Constable Jurgensen asks Renée.

"No. Of course not."

"So you don't know?" he snaps.

"No. I mean of course he doesn't own a gun."

"How can you be so sure?"

"I know my brother. He isn't violent."

"But he paints tanks."

"Because he's making a comment on war!"

Constable Wilson murmurs something into Jurgensen's ear and he nods back.

"Fine. That will be all. But you tell Attila we'll need to see him for questioning."

"Maybe you should talk to Madame X, instead," Renée says. Mistake number seven. The more Renée argues, the guiltier Attila seems.

"We've already spoken to her," Constable Wilson answers.

"We'll be in touch," Constable Jurgensen says. He waves a few fingers in goodbye.

"Bye, kids," Constable Wilson calls, smiling like she's still on our side.

DAY ONE, MISTAKE EIGHT

"Why did you tell them to question Madame X?" I ask Renée after we leave the office. "She likes kids and dogs. A perfectly nice lady."

"Because she said she hated those fish. And she's wearing a big coat and it's not even cold."

"You think she was hiding all 250 fish in her coat?"

"Quiet in the hall!" a teacher calls from a classroom and slams her door.

Renée rolls her eyes and shrugs.

I lower my voice. "She thanked us for taking them down. Why would she say that if she stole them herself?"

"Oh, that's just to throw us off track. She says they block her vision. She can't see the" — Renée forms air quotes with her finger — "'keedies.'"

"But Attila hates them more. He can't even go close to one of those fish without smoke coming out of his ears."

"Oh, you're just like them. You want to pin every crime on Attila."

Mrs. Worsley pokes her head outside of our classroom now and waves us back. "Stephen, Renée, quit lollygagging in the hall!"

"Later!" Renée hisses. She looks as though she's bursting with other stuff she wants to say.

At lunchtime, over her jam and cream cheese bagel, she finally explodes. "You don't understand, Stephen. If the police show up at my door to question Attila, the fighting will start again. My father will yell. My mother will cry."

That makes me feel bad for Renée. I swallow a bite of my own cream cheese sandwich. "Maybe you should text him," I tell her. "Get him to go to the police by himself."

"Hmm." She thinks a moment. "You're right. That way, my parents won't have to know." She pulls out her cell, keys in a long message, and then looks up. "Now, you know what we have to do?"

"No, what?"

"We have to find the real thief so we can prove Attila's innocence."

"Aren't you forgetting something?" I ask.

"What?"

"The real thief probably has a gun."

After lunch we sit through a class on metaphors and similes, which is as much fun as a barrel of puppies. (That's a simile, by the way.) Mrs. Worsley passes around a box, and we have to write down two nouns and drop them in. I throw in *fish* and *dogs*.

When everyone's put theirs in, we get to pull out two. I get *bomb* and *Minecraft* but Mrs. Worsley lets me choose another one because she says brand names are not allowed. I get *mistake* this time.

"Now, class, I want you to write a couple of sentences using either a metaphor or a simile."

Renée gets *alien* and *brother*, and she reads out this sentence: "My brother has turned into an alien. I don't even know what planet he's from."

I agree with her there.

"Good!" Mrs. Worsley points to Tyson.

"I got *art* and *gun*," he answers. "I can't think of anything."

"Class, help him out!"

Renée calls out, "Art is a gun that fires everyone up."

"Excellent. Raise your hand next time! Stephen?"

Mine makes me feel a bit squishy inside. "A mistake is a bomb that goes off when you least expect it."

"Hmm, very nice," Mrs. Worsley says.

No, it's not nice at all, I think. Seven mistake bombs have already exploded in front of me today.

Finally, it's time to pack up for home. As we write last-minute notes in our agenda, Mrs. Worsley hands us each an envelope with an explanation of the lockdown. But she says we are not to look at it without a parent.

Of course, Renée and I already know about the gunman. She's always afraid of being alone and likes to hang around with me until someone's home at her house. Today, she's even more clingy.

By now all the recycling bins and garbage pails are empty, and all the furniture, the toy kitchen, and that cool painting of the boy and his rabbit are gone.

When we get to our house, Dad is sitting on the couch knitting something tiny in pale blue. On four needles, no less.

A strange smile creeps over Renée's face. "Well, hi, Mr. Noble. Whatcha making?"

"Hi, kids. A sweater." He holds up the knitting so we can see it better.

Renée looks at me with wide eyes.

Oh, no, she can't possibly think my mom's expecting a baby. Then, for a moment, I panic. *Is Mom pregnant?* "It's pretty tiny, Dad."

He nods. "The Yorkies are. I'm knitting one for each. Their owner wants them in the colours of the rainbow."

Renée's mouth drops open. "You mean, she has seven dogs?"

"No, five. I'm going to trim the necklines with the other two colours. Indigo and orange. Mrs. Irwin was very specific." He shrugs his shoulder. "She's an artist."

"Wow, that looks really hard to do, Dad. How do you know it will fit?"

"I measured. But this is the test sweater," he answers.

I drop my backpack so I can haul out Mrs. Watier's note to parents. "Dad, something happened at school today."

"You two aren't in trouble, are you?"

"No, no. But there was a lockdown. Here, read this."

Dad puts his knitting down and takes the letter. His eyebrows crush together as he scans it. For a while after, he just stares at it, and then he looks up at us. "So you know you were safe at all times. They found a gun in the library and needed to be very cautious."

"Just the gun, no gunman?" Renée asks.

"That's right. They locked down the school because they thought whoever left it there might still be in the building. They were wrong. That person had left."

I picture Mr. Rupert scouting through the school in a camouflage uniform, both hands in front of him, holding a gun. I know when he sees me on his camera delivering the newspaper, he's going to think I stole his mailbox. "Things have gone missing in the neighbourhood," I finally say.

"A Halloween display, a mailbox, and the Stream of Dreams project from our school," Renée adds.

"Still why would anyone put a gun in our library?" I ask. "Do you think it's a warning?"

"Put or leave?" Dad says.

The phone rings before I get a chance to really think about the difference. Dad takes the call in the kitchen, but I can tell it's Mom on the other end by his happy tone of voice. She's in London, probably at the airport. Dad lowers his voice now, so I can't make out what he's saying. Then, finally, he calls me. "Stephen, Mom's on the line."

I dash to the phone. "Hi, Mom!"

"Hi, Stephen. Lots of excitement at school again, I hear."

"Yeah, the police even questioned us. Wanted to know if we saw someone suspicious around the school."

"Did you?"

"I don't know." I think about the teenager with the diamond stud nose ring, Mr. Rupert, the crossing guard … "What does suspicious even look like?"

"Good question," Mom says. "You know, when I used to fly up north, security once found a hand grenade in a passenger's carry-on."

"Really?" My stomach turns queasy at the thought. Flying makes me nervous even without weapons going on board.

"Yup. They stopped a young man. Turns out he was a filmmaker and it was a prop. Delayed the flight by an hour."

"Do you think someone's making a film in my school?" I ask.

"No. I'm saying there may be a good explanation for the gun. But I'm glad your principal played it safe, just like I'm glad security searched that man's bag." I can hear the smile in my mom's voice, and I feel as though she's hugged me even though she isn't in the room.

For a moment I just hold on to the feeling. Then another worry bubbles up inside me and I have to share it with Mom. "Mr. Rupert's mailbox was stolen ..." Maybe Mom can make me feel better about him. He's scary.

But that turns out to be mistake number eight of the day.

"Mr. Rupert? Oh, no. Please don't touch any of his stuff, ever. Since his wife died, he hasn't been the same.... Listen to me, Stephen? I have to board the plane now. I love you."

"Love you, too. But Mom?"

Click!

"Bye!" I say to dead air.

Even when she's away, Mom calls me to stay in touch and to calm me down sometimes. So this is Mom's mistake. Number eight of the day. Warning me that Mr. Rupert hasn't been the same since his wife died definitely does not make me feel better.

DAY ONE, MISTAKE NINE

Back in the family room, Renée holds two knitting needles in her hands and Dad demonstrates how to cast on. "Once you get the knack of it, you'll find it can be really relaxing. I used knitting to help me quit smoking."

Mr. Rupert hasn't been the same as what? I seriously need relaxing. "Do you have a couple of needles for me?" I ask.

"Sure. You could make a rainbow-coloured scarf. I'm not going to use all of the third ball I bought for each of the dogs." He passes me some pale-blue yarn.

I already know how to cast on the first row of stitches. But I make my loops way too tight. When he shows us how to knit the next row, it's a struggle for me.

"Hold the wool a little looser. See how Renée does it."

She smiles and holds up her two needles so I can see better. Her fingers fly. She's already on her second row.

Dad returns to his own project.

"Dad, do you think Mr. Rupert has a gun?"

"What?" His needles click together. "Why?" *Click!* "No!" *Click!*

"He's an army kind of guy. And Mom says he hasn't been the same since his wife died."

Click, click, click. The needles move quicker. "I don't think he'd go into a school with a gun because he's sad about his wife, if that's what you're getting at."

"No. But he wants to get even with the person who stole his mailbox."

"That mailbox was really special." Dad slows down on the knitting. "It looked exactly like their house."

"Mr. Rupert said he's going to look at his surveillance camera to find the thief."

"Well, good luck to him. Even if he can make him out on the video, he still has to find him."

"Or her," Renée pipes in.

"What if he knows the person, and he, or she, goes to our school?" I ask.

"I think he would definitely go to your principal. I don't think he would chase anyone with a gun."

"My father told me that Mr. Rupert's in the reserve. He went on a military exercise," Renée says, "and the two teams fought each other with real guns!"

Dad frowns and knits more quickly again. "I'm sure the weapons only used blanks." *Click, click.*

"But that's a military exercise. It doesn't make him a gun nut."

The frantic clicking makes me think even Dad is worried.

One thing is true, for sure. Mr. Rupert is definitely a dog- and kid-hating nut.

Beethoven's Fifth plays from Renée's backpack and she checks her cellphone. "Attila went to the police station so he's going to be home late."

Dad's head jerks up and the clicking stops entirely.

"He's just going in for some questioning. *Volunteering* to go," I add so Dad doesn't think he's in trouble again.

"Well, that's good. That he's volunteering. The police are here to help us. And if we can help them solve a crime, we should."

I try not to think about Dad's statement too hard. Instead, I concentrate on my knitting. My stitches are still too tight. I throw down the needles. "Maybe we should walk Ping and Pong now. Who knows when Attila will get home."

Dad looks up from the tiny blue sweater growing from his needles. "Would you like to stay for supper, Renée? We're having meat loaf and sweet potato fries. A salad if Stephen makes it."

"Yes, please."

"Okay," I tell her. "Then let's go to the Bennetts' now and get the dogs."

We head out the door, down a couple of long blocks, and cross the street. Ping is jumping up and down in front of the picture window already. Pong's head appears. His long tail wags behind him. I grab the key from my pocket and open the door.

There's nothing better than how happy those dogs get as we step inside. Ping barks at us as he dashes around. Pong moves more slowly, leaning against me for pats.

I rattle the treat bag to get them to sit and hold still as we snap on the leashes.

Then out we go. They know where we're going. We cross the street and they pull and wag. Their mouths hang open and they breathe a happy *huh, huh, huh* as we turn the corner and head along the sidewalk in the direction of Brant Hills Park.

I can't help looking at the empty recycling bins lined up along the walkway and wishing I could have rescued that play cooking station or at least the painting with the rabbit.

Who throws art away? I check out the house that belongs to that recycling bin. A movement at the side catches my eyes. Squeezed between the hedge and the fence is a mass of wriggling brown fur — it looks like a pile of small moppy animals. They leap on top of each other as though trying to escape over the fence.

Ping barks frantically, Pong strains at the leash.

"Awwww. Puppies!" Renée cries.

But then, they seem to knock into each other and things get ugly. They yap, they snarl, they hiss, they growl. They snap at each other. One of them yelps.

A woman's voice calls out from a window. "Hush now! Stop!"

They roll around, still growling and snapping.

"Oh, no!" I say. "They're Yorkies."

"Your father's customers?"

"I think so."

A woman comes to the fence and scoops up two tiny wiggling dogs. "Stop it, Blue. Sit, Rose. Goldie, quiet!"

Named for the colours of the rainbow. Cute. "Come on, let's go!" I pull Pong away.

Renée picks up Ping.

We cross Duncaster and Renée sets Ping back down. From there, the dogs pull hard toward our school. Behind it lies Brant Hills Park. The dogs gallop together and we run after them. Pong looks happy as he doubles around and bows to Ping, inviting him to play. Ping bows back and they zigzag. Big and small, quiet and loud, still somehow they have become buddies.

Right now they've tangled up their leashes. Renée drops Ping's so we can detangle, but we're not quick enough. Ping makes his break, dragging Pong along.

There's no one around. No skateboarders on the path, no squirrels anywhere, no little kids with ice cream. The world seems safe from them. They run to the fence on the other side and Pong squats to do his business.

"Hey. You kids." Behind a fence, a lady with frosted white hair points with her cigar. Mr. Ron's mom — Mr. Ron was our old crossing guard. "You gonna clean that up?"

"Yes, ma'am. My bags are right here." I pat a pocket in my cargo pants, then take a bag out, bend, and scoop up the pile.

"Say, I remember you kids." She's wearing the same flowered muumuu as the last time we saw her, only she's draped a puffy red coat over her shoulders. "See you got your dogs back all right."

Last time she warned us about a family of raccoons a second too late. Pong and Ping yanked the leashes out of our hands to chase them. Pong disappeared for a couple of days until Ping led us to Jessie's old pool house, where a dognapper had been keeping him.

"How's Mr. Ron?" Renée asks. "Does he miss us?"

"Yup, yup, yup. Bigger fish to fry now, though." *Hurh, hurh, hurh!* Mr. Ron's mom laughs like a car trying to start in winter.

Renée and I look at each other when it doesn't seem like she can stop. Finally, she sputters out. Smoking those cigars can't be any good for her throat.

"Speaking of fish," Renée says, "did you see anything strange happening at the school last night? Someone took all the Stream of Dreams fish off the fence."

"Just the usual. Bunch of teenagers in the back of the school. You know. Hangin' out and whatnot, with their tools."

"What kind of tools?" Renée asks.

"I don't know. Hammers? Wire cutters?" Mr. Ron's mom puffs on her cigar as she thinks. "There were four of them."

"You didn't see them working on the fence by the kindergarten door?" I ask.

"Nah. Can't see that far," she answers.

"They didn't walk back with a bag of stuff? Painted fish?" Renée asks.

"Dunno. Only smoke one Habano a night." She holds up her cigar.

"Did you see if one of them had a mohawk?" I ask.

Renée fixes me with her death-ray stare. I know, I know, she does not want the criminal to be Attila. She hates it when anyone even thinks anything bad about her brother. Is this her mistake or mine, though? Number nine of the day. I should be loyal to her and pretend Attila is the saint she wants him to be. But then we wouldn't get a valuable piece of information.

"Couldn't tell. They were wearing black caps."

DAY ONE, MISTAKE TEN

We say goodbye and leave, and to be safe, I change the subject. We're close to the Brant Hills library and community centre and I remember about looking for *The Night Gardener*. "Renée, could you hold the dogs so I can get that book the teacher's reading to us?"

"Ooooh. The creepy one. Yeah! Maybe I can read it after."

"Okay. Why don't you go into the tennis court with them where we can shut the gate?"

"C'mon. I can handle them. Besides, what if some tennis players come?"

People with rackets and tennis balls — she has a point. So instead, I tie Pong's leash to the bench and Renée sits down with Ping in her arms. I dash into the building.

The hallway between the library and the gym acts as a game centre. There's an air hockey game, a foosball table and a Ping-Pong table. A couple of toddlers twirl and rattle the handles of the foosball people, and a mom and a little girl push around the puck on the air hockey table. But they're just fooling around.

At the Ping-Pong table, things look more intense. On either side, two old guys duel, batting the

Ping-Pong ball back and forth. Crouched over the table, cap pulled low over his head, Mr. Kowalski, the hundred-year-old jogger, looks different today, less scrunched up. At least his body does. His face looks all screwed together in concentration. He slams the ball across the table. Whoa!

The other guy smacks it right back.

And whack! *Pick-pock.* Back again! *Pick-pock.* I love that sound.

I want to watch but I can't leave Renée by herself with both Ping and Pong. After all, I'm the professional dog walker. I scoot into the library and look for the book. *A* for Auxier, Jonathan. It's in the junior fiction department: one copy, tree on the cover, creepy top-hat guy with a watering can in the tree. Yay! I grab it and check it out.

On my way to the door, a bright-fuchsia poster on the community bulletin board catches my eye. *Celebrate Burlington with Art!* the header reads, in royal-blue letters. Burlington landmarks — the Skyway bridge, the pier, city hall, and the art gallery itself — surround the letters. Any kind of painting, sculpture, or installation that's Burlington-inspired can be entered. The entries will be displayed at the gallery. First prize includes a partial scholarship to an arts program and a possible exhibition. There's also a people's choice award of five hundred dollars. But wait a minute … I check my phone for the date … the deadline is tomorrow. Probably too late for Attila to enter. I snap a picture of it anyway and message it to Renée.

Then I head back outside.

Ping and Pong surround someone in a hoodie who has stooped to admire them. Someone who is wearing leggings with water lilies.

"Awwww!" she croons. "Cute." Tucked under her arm are a few oversized hardcover books. Hoodie girl has been to the library, too.

"The little one likes to kiss people," I warn the girl as she stoops to pat Ping.

"Aw! I don't mind."

Yeah, yeah, people think dogs who lick your face are so cute. But Ping likes to stick his tongue right in your mouth if it's open, or even worse, up your nose. "Down, Ping!"

Sometimes, he gets so enthusiastic, he may add a little nibble. "Ping, NO!" He appears too enthusiastic today. I try to pat him down but miss, and instead he makes an incredible little dog leap to reach her face.

"*Owwwwww!*" She drops her books with a clunk, cupping her hands to her nose.

My head swirls. Blood doesn't usually make me sick, but it's pooling around the stud in her nose, dripping through her fingers. I shut my eyes.

"Is that your blood or the dog's?" Renée calls.

I force my eyes open again.

Renée drops down. "C'mere, boy." She grabs Ping's muzzle and checks his mouth. "Are you hurt?" She's being her usual unsympathetic self to any human who's not Attila.

"Are *you* all right?" I ask the hoodie girl.

"No. The dog ripped my nose." This sounds like an annoyed voice, not one in pain.

"Well, that's your own fault," Renée snaps. "Even little kids know enough to ask first before patting a dog."

"Renée! Stop!" I can't believe her. I turn to the girl. "I'm sorry." I reach into another of my pockets. Ever since Ping pushed a skateboarder over, I keep some emergency first aid supplies on me. Inside, there's an antiseptic wipe in a little pouch. I tear it open. "Here, let me …" I dab at the blood on her nose. "Maybe you should take your thingie out."

"No, I can't. The hole will close up."

"Ping cut his tongue!" Renée reports. Pong crowds around her, too, wanting to help investigate.

"I don't know how I can bandage your nose if you keep the sparkly stone in." I frown up at her.

"Here, give me that!" The girl dabs at the wound, now. "I'm not going to bandage my nose. Are you crazy?"

That's when I recognize her. She's the one who took that ugly fish plaque from the recycling.

"Did that dog have his rabies shots?" she asks.

"Of course," I answer.

"Have you had a tetanus shot?" Renée asks her.

I kick Renée and signal her with my eyes. *Be nice!* This could be so bad. If hoodie girl reports Ping to Animal Control, the Bennetts will be unhappy with Noble Dog Walking. But worse, Ping could be labelled a dangerous dog. No leash-free parks, a muzzle on him whenever he's in public …

"He's a very affectionate animal," I say. "He didn't mean to hurt you."

"He hurt his tongue on your nose stud," Renée grumbles.

"Let me give you my business card," I tell her. Dad wants me to take responsibility for my mistakes. "If you have any um … medical costs, we'll cover them." I give her a Noble Dog Walking card.

"Probably need a new stud," she says in a nasal voice. The blood seems to have stopped but she's still pressing the wipe to her nose.

"Maybe something less lethal this time," Renée suggests. "Can a vet even stitch up a dog's tongue?"

Can a doctor stitch up a nose? "Look. We're very sorry," I continue. "It wasn't a real diamond, was it?" How much will a new stud cost? I wonder. Dad will kill me.

She shakes her head. "Is the puppy okay?"

On cue, Ping flips over on his back, offering up a pink-and-black spotted belly.

If she stoops again to pat him, I'll know all is forgiven.

She does not stoop, however, not even to pick up her books. Instead, she waves the card. "I'll let you know."

I bend down and pick up her Vincent Van Gogh and Renaissance painters books and hand them to her. She just grabs them and walks away.

Then I crouch to check out Ping. I can feel Pong's long tail flopping against my back. "There's a bit of blood on his incisor. I don't see a cut on his tongue."

"That's because there is none," Renée says. "I just said that to make her feel bad. Like anything could."

"Really," I say, patting Pong and Ping at the same time. "You were alone five minutes with the dogs …"

"It wasn't our fault. She's the one who stopped to pat them."

"So? The dog's not supposed to leap up and rip open her nose!" I snap.

Renée rolls her eyes. "You were here by then. You could have stopped Ping, too."

She's right — she always is — which doesn't stop her from being annoying. "Could you have at least been a little nicer? The girl's blood is on Ping's tooth!"

"Oh, her nose jewellery always gets caught on everything. Besides, she was never very nice to Attila."

"What do you mean?"

"Her name is Star and she was Attila's girlfriend till last month."

"Ohhhhh! Now I get it. So you have a hate-on for her?"

"She's the one who got him into trouble all the time. She suggested the tank on Champlain High's wall. Then she took off when the cops came."

"Still, Renée, if she reports Ping, it would be awful. Dogs don't get a lot of chances with this stuff. Sometimes, not even one."

"Which is why I wanted her to think Ping is injured. To let her know this is all because of her!"

"All right. Let's just go." I am not going to change her mind and what's done is done. "Home," I tell Pong. He reluctantly turns around.

Ping does his miniature mule routine. Stubborn, refusing to listen, digging his paws in. "Just pick him up, Renée. He has to obey!"

She scoops him up and the two of them give me almost the same look. Those slivers of white at the sides of Ping's eyes make him seem just as angry as Renée.

"You were gone a long time," Renée grumbles as we head back to the Bennetts' house.

I ignore her complaint. "Did you get my text about the art contest?"

"No, I didn't." She puts Ping down to check her phone. She scrolls to my message. "I think Attila may have entered this already. I'll send it to him, just in case."

"You're welcome," I say.

"You're welcome back. For watching the dogs," she snaps. "Did you get the book, at least?"

I hold it up. By now, I know I should loan it to her first to patch things up between us. But I don't.

We keep walking, no one saying much. The dogs don't even mark anything on the way back. In the house, they each just head for their beds and slump down. Pong gives a long one-note whine as we head for the door.

Beethoven's Fifth plays from Renée's phone. Probably means her brother is home. She can skip supper at our place, which could give us some cooling-off time.

Mistake number ten of the day. Of course, I'm wrong about the message. Attila is still at the police station. But the bigger mistake was advising him to go to the police for questioning in the first place.

They've arrested him.

For theft and possession of a firearm.

DAY ONE, MISTAKE ELEVEN

"Did the police actually find a gun on Attila? 'Cause our school gunman left his weapon behind."

"How should I know?" Renée snaps. "Mr. Rupert reported Attila to the police because he saw him on his surveillance camera. And Mr. Rupert's gun is missing."

"*Really*?" The word comes out on a high note, with all my relief and delight singing through. Mr. Rupert won't be hunting me down for the missing mailbox. Not if he's pegged Attila for the crime.

Renée scowls at me.

I try again, using a lower, more worried tone. "I mean, really?" We start walking again.

"Yes. Apparently the camera caught him with the mailbox in his hands."

"Gee. He's lucky the police have him and not Mr. Rupert. Things could have gone way worse."

Renée hangs her head.

"What about the gun?" I ask. "That's really a serious crime."

"I don't know," Renée wails.

Whoops, I shouldn't have reminded her.

"There's going to be so much yelling at home."

"You know what? Let's ask Dad if you can sleep over."

That perks Renée up a little.

When we arrive back at the house, I start making the salad right away to butter Dad up. I even slice olives because I know he likes them. Renée chops onions and cries; I'm not sure if they're onion tears or not.

Dad uses two forks to flip over each sweet potato fry, then shoves the baking sheet back in the oven.

"Would it be all right if Renée stays the night? Her parents have something important to take care of."

"In the middle of the week?" Dad says.

"We can do our homework together."

Dad knows how smart Renée is but he just keeps staring at us. His mouth buckles but he does not want to give in, I can tell.

"My brother's going to jail," Renée moans. Her moan and possibly the onion tears finally win Dad over.

"All right. Call your mother," he says. "Stephen, why don't you check that the sheets are on the guest bed. And see if you can find an old T-shirt and some sweatpants for Renée to wear to bed."

Renée gets the all-clear from her mom while I scramble through a bag of giveaway clothes in my closet. Then we both head for the guest bedroom, where we see it.

The painting from the recycling bin — the one with the rabbit and the boy in the snow — as if by magic — hangs over the bed now.

"Wow. Your dad must have taken it from the curb!"

I tilt my head, take in the powder-blue sky against the sleepy whiteness of the snow, and inhale deeply. So calming. I release my breath. Then I focus on the charcoal-grey rabbit and the boy looking over the whole scene, almost the way I am. Does it make him feel peaceful, too? The signature scrawled in the right-hand corner catches my eye. It's hard to make out, but I think I can see a loopy *K* and *O* and something that could be a *W*.

Renée leans over the bed and squints at that corner now, too. "Kowalski — W. Kowalski," she reads out loud.

I tilt my head the other way. "Do you think it's our hundred-year-old jogger?"

She straightens and punches my arm. "Stop calling him that! Of course it's him. His first name is William."

"Sorry, it's just I keep seeing him running and he does look … old."

"He's also Attila's portfolio tutor. And he's not even sixty-five. He has osteoporosis."

"Really?" Of course she would know exactly why he jogs hunched over. I don't even know what that word means. "He plays a really intense game of Ping-Pong."

"He's passionate about everything he does. Least that's what Attila says." Her face droops as she mentions her brother's name.

Luckily, Dad calls up the stairs at that moment. "The sheets on the bed must be the same ones you slept in last time you stayed over." We hear his footsteps up, then his head appears at the door. "No need to change them … Oh, do you like my new painting?"

"We love it," I answer. "We saw it near a recycling bin this morning but didn't have time to rescue it."

"My client threw it out. The Yorkies' owner."

Renée shakes her head. "Throwing out art, that just seems wrong."

Dad nods. "She was in charge of redecorating her staff lounge. Says it no longer fit the decor."

"You think she could find another place to hang it, in the halls, or …" I hesitate.

"Give it away," Renée finishes my sentence.

"I agree." Dad shrugs. "But she seemed almost angry with it. Maybe she has a beef with the painter."

"Well," — I can't help smiling — "at least you saved it."

"It makes the whole room cozy." Renée smiles, too.

"So I didn't find a bookshelf, but this art found a home." Dad folds his arms across his chest.

We all look at it for an extra moment.

When his watch beeps, Dad finally backs away. "Supper's ready."

"Great," I answer. "I'm starved."

We follow Dad downstairs to the kitchen to eat.

What Dad's homemade liver bites are to dogs, his meat loaf is to me. Irresistible. I'd sit, stay, shake paw, anything to have it. Maybe he even puts some of the same ingredients in it. Alongside the meat loaf, the sweet potato fries look crisp and perfect. "Dad, you've outdone yourself!"

"Mmm, you make a very good salad, too." Renée closes her eyes as she tastes another forkful. When she gives a compliment, she really means it.

"Thanks. It's the goat cheese. Always works well with the olives. And I find dairy so de-stressing."

When we're done supper, Renée and I work on math problems.

"I really don't get estimating. I mean, what's the point when your cellphone has a calculator?"

"You're training your mind, Renée. And like Mrs. Worsley explained, it's a way of double-checking numbers, in case you press a button twice on your phone or something."

"I guess. Can we play Dancing Resolution now?"

"Dancing Resolution?" I repeat, stalling for time. I want to bowl on the game station instead. It's probably the only sport I'm good at. My old best friend, Jessie, would have played Wii bowling with me. "You really want to dance?"

Renée's eyes moonsize and she nods frantically.

I have no sense of rhythm and I find following the moves hard; dancing makes me feel stupid. On the other hand, when my Wii bowling ball smashes against those white pins, the sound shouts out that I am a winner.

But today Renée needs to forget about her troublemaking brother for a while. So instead, I become a manga-style hip-hop avatar with stick-up hair, a muscle shirt, sweatpants, and sneakers.

She becomes a Wonder Woman–type girl with a long black ponytail, tall white boots, and a short bright-red dress.

For an hour or so, we could be the coolest kids in the school with our moves. Although we're probably the geekiest. Renée beats me by a couple hundred points, and by the time Dad reminds us that it's a school night and we need to get our eight hours sleep, she looks pretty happy. I let her have the bathroom first, thinking we can forget about missing mailboxes, fish, doll corpses, guns, and especially the fact that Attila might be responsible for it all. I lie back in my bed, tired and relaxed. My eyes close.

It feels like I've been asleep for only a few moments when Renée shakes my shoulder.

It can't be morning already. "What time is it?" I mumble.

"Almost midnight," she whispers.

"Go back to bed. You can tell me about whatever you want in the morning."

Last mistake of the day, it's a bonus one, number eleven, becomes trying to tell Renée to wait for anything.

"No, no!" She drags me by the arm. "You have to see this!"

day two

THE GREAT MISTAKE

MYSTERIES

DAY TWO, MISTAKE ONE

Renée drags me to the window. "Look over there!" She points, knocking me in the nose in the process.

"What am I supposed to be seeing?" I ask, blinking sleep from my eyes.

"Over there by the parking lot. The kids with the wagon." She grabs my chin and turns my head.

Once I look in the right direction, I can make out what looks like three teenagers dressed in black from their caps to their sneakers. One hunches over a wagon. The lights over the lot cast them in a crazy glow. "Oh my gosh. They have Grumpy!"

"That's what the statue in their wagon is?" Renée asks.

"Yeah! Quick, take a picture."

Renée grabs for her cellphone, raises it to the window.

"Grumpy belongs to the Lebels next door," I explain as she clicks away. "Mrs. Lebel bought him when Mr. Lebel complained about cleaning the pool all the time."

Renée checks the screen on her phone. "No good. The flash bounces off the window." She frowns.

"Call the cops, then!"

"No, no. They'll be gone by time they arrive. Let's follow them ourselves!"

Now if we were watching this in a movie, we'd both call out to the actors, "Don't do it! They'll kill you!" But instead, because I'm half-asleep, the idea sounds really good. We don't even change out of our pajamas, figuring there's no time, really. Not if we want to see where they go.

"Shh!" I say as we tiptoe downstairs. We slide into our sneakers near the door. I open the closet and we both freeze when the hinge creaks. *One thousand, two thousand, three thousand*, I count in my head. No sign of Dad getting up. I toss Renée her jacket and throw my own over my pajamas.

I open the front door. No sound, so we dash.

"We need to go through the backyard if we don't want to lose them," Renée says.

"You mean climb over the fence?" I ask.

"It's the fastest way. If we take the sidewalk around the block to the parking lot, they'll be gone."

Again, this sounds like a great idea at 12:15 in the morning. "Okay," I agree and we run through the backyard to the fence.

Neither of us is any good at gym, or climbing, for that matter. I try to hoist Renée up by giving her my cupped hands as a step. She makes it to the top of the fence, and then, as she attempts to swing her leg over, gets her sweatpants hooked on a wire.

My sneakers stick in the wire diamonds, so I have to pull my feet out of them and scramble up in bare feet. I unhook Renée, but then catch my own pajamas. "Ow!" The wire scratches my thigh and my pants tear open as gravity throws me over the rest of the way. Now, the pajama material flaps in the breeze, and I stand on the cold field with no shoes. My teeth chatter as I try to pull my sneakers through the fence. No use. Not happening.

"Oh, just come on!" Renée says. "They're getting away."

Easy for her to say.

The grass feels prickly on the soles of my feet in some places and squishy in others. I hop, step, and move as fast as I can, but it's no use. The three of them have disappeared.

"Ohhh," Renée groans. "Where did they go?"

"The shortcut?" I suggest as I huddle and shiver. "Or …"

"Or what?"

"Maybe they ducked into one of the houses right across the street."

We both stand and stare. From somewhere I hear barking. "The Yorkies?" I ask.

"Seriously, Stephen. You can tell one bark from another?"

"No, but they live over there. Mrs. Irwin is an artist," I add as if that means anything.

"You think those thieves live with your dad's client?"

"I dunno." But a thought is forming. It's late at night or early in the morning, depending on how you look at it. The thought feels like a storm cloud gathering in my brain. "By any chance, did you notice if any of them wore a nose ring?"

"Honestly, no."

I shake my head. "So we can't even know if Star is one of them."

"No. But at least Attila can't be involved! He's still in custody."

"Just because he didn't steal Grumpy doesn't mean he didn't take the mailbox. I mean, he was caught on video."

"Yes, but there's a perfectly good explanation for it all."

"Okay, what?"

"I don't know — I haven't heard it, yet."

"Uh-huh."

"Well, he won't say a word to the police, of course. I think he's protecting someone." Renée glares at me like she's daring me to disagree.

I don't; what's the point? "Look, can we just go? I'm freezing. And I still have to get my sneakers from the fence."

"Wait a minute, I see something!" She jogs over

to the parking lot and picks up a black cap. "One of them dropped their hat."

"That's great," I say as I start heading back to the fence. "You think the cops will identify the perps with the DNA?"

"Maybe Troy can sniff them out."

I roll my eyes and keep walking.

"Wait! We're not climbing back over. You're injured," Renée says.

"What if someone sees us?" I ask as she pulls me the other way.

"At this hour? Come on. Who would be out now, except maybe another crook?"

I stop and pull away from her. "That doesn't make me feel too good."

"Oh, don't worry so much! Let's just go by Duncaster and Cavendish."

You overanalyze everything, Mom always says. I know I do. And worrying is just another way I do that. Maybe I should knit a few rows before I go to bed since that works for Dad.

It's late, too, and my brain doesn't want to work so hard. I end up just following after Renée as she cuts through the parking lot. My feet have developed hard hooves of mud by now so they're numb. Walking fast keeps me warm.

This definitely becomes mistake number one of the day.

By the time we get to the sidewalk, I hear a familiar cannon-shot voice.

"Hey, you! What are you doing out here?" Mr. Rupert skulks through the parking lot toward us!

We break into a run.

DAY TWO, MISTAKE TWO

Did I mention we're not good at gym? That's because not only are we not great at climbing, neither of us can run very fast. Mr. Rupert should be able to catch us. But I don't look back. It would slow me down, and I'd see him closing in on us and freeze.

So I pump my arms and legs, hard as I can. The cement of the sidewalk sands the mud from my feet. The wind blows out my pajama pants like sails. "Have to keep running, keep running, keep running," I tell myself even though I just want to roll up in a ball.

Being tiny, Renée zips ahead. Maybe I can at least delay Mr. Rupert so she can get away.

"C'mon, Stephen! Don't slow down."

"Okay, okay. Faster, faster," I tell myself. Terror gives me speed.

By the time we reach the corner, my gums pound from the blood rushing to them. My chest aches, my shins splint. "You keep going." I wave Renée on. "Save yourself!"

"Don't be such a drama king." She grabs my arm and yanks me along. We make the turn on to Cavendish.

That's when I finally see. No one is following us.

"Hey, he's gone!" I tell Renée and slow down.

"Good, great!" She stops and doubles over to catch her breath.

"What do you think he's doing out here?" I ask.

Hanging upside down like that makes her smile look funny. "I heard a rumour that he's seeing Mrs. Klein."

"Ha, ha, ha. Good one. Can you picture that?"

She straightens and shrugs. "Maybe. Question is, why did he stop running?"

"He's chasing a couple of kids in pajamas," I tell her. "That would look bad to anyone driving by."

"Well, good thing. Let's go home."

"As soon as I catch my breath." My heart finally stops pounding into my mouth and we move again more slowly. The long way home takes longer, and when we get back, both of us tug at the sneakers in the fence. "If we had wire cutters, we could just cut them free," Renée says.

Finally, when I fold the toe, I manage to get the shoe loose. Renée removes the other one the same way. We sneak back into the house, up the stairs, and wave good night to each other so as not to wake up Dad. With a little bit of luck, no one will ever know about the nighttime detective work that didn't produce any leads.

Next morning, I sleep through my alarm and Dad shakes me awake. "You guys obviously stayed up too late," he says as I drag myself out of bed. He knocks long and hard on the guest bedroom to get Renée up, too.

We eat a quick bowl of granola with strawberry yogurt and then head off to walk Ping and Pong. As they leap all over us and we snap on their leashes, I notice something in Renée's hands.

"You've got to be kidding! That's never going to work."

"Bloodhounds can do it," Renée says as she bends down, "so why not greyhounds, right, Pong?" She holds out the black knitted cap we found in the parking lot.

Ping snatches it away in a toothy grin and shakes it like he needs to kill it.

I roll my eyes at Renée as she pries it from his mouth. When we step outside with them, she lets both dogs sniff it again.

"It's not like we can let them loose to find the owner," I say.

"Just let them guide the leash," Renée says. "Not so tight." She touches my arm.

I have to chase Pong as he lopes along. "They're just going to take us to the park. That's where they always want to go."

Renée runs, too, to keep up with Ping. But they don't turn toward Brant Hills; they seem to want us to go across the street, back to the shortcut.

A squirrel dashes in front of us and throws Ping off the scent for a moment. He yanks Renée's arm almost out of its socket. "Ow! Stop!" Renée calls as she pulls him back. She holds the hat out to Pong again, and the two dogs lead us along past Mrs. Whittingham's to a house that looks a lot like the Bennetts'.

"They think they're home," I suggest as they pull us toward the door.

Renée shakes her head. "Uh-uh. This is where Star lives. Give them a treat, they've done well."

I reach into my pocket, and instantly Ping and Pong sit down, ears up in a salute to Dad's liver bites.

"Let's ring the bell, see what Star says." Renée reaches for the white push-bar at the side of the door.

In the light of day after a few hours of sleep, I'm much smarter, or maybe more anxious. "I don't think this is a good idea at all."

Too late. She presses and we hear chimes, foot poundings, and a cheery, "I'll get it!"

The door swings open. Too late to run. The dogs begin wagging. It's her — the girl with the diamond nose stud, Star. Except now she wears a gold ring and leggings with big pink roses. Imagine, she went out with Attila. She looks so much brighter and hotter, I think.

"Oh, it's you guys." She puts her hands out so Ping won't jump up on her again.

"How's your nose?" I ask.

"It's okay. Thanks for asking."

"Did you lose this?" Renée demands and thrusts out the black cap.

"Um, not sure. I have one like it …"

She's stalling, I can tell.

"Where did you find it?" Star asks.

"At Brant Hills Park," Renée answers. "Last night."

"I dunno. Could be. I bought mine at the Dollarama so there are lots out there like it."

"Really? Let me ask you this. Where were you last night at midnight?"

"Um. Asleep," she answers.

"No, you weren't. You were transporting a stolen lawn ornament across Brant Hills. We saw you." Renée stares straight into Star's eyes as she bluffs.

"No, you didn't." Star stares right back.

"Oh, no? Well, then when the police run a DNA test on this hat, they won't find anything like a hair of yours on it, right?" As she says this, she snatches at Star's shoulder. Star smacks her hand away.

Renée raises up a closed hand with her thumb and forefinger poking out as though they are holding a strand of hair. "Nothing that will match this one?"

"You don't have any hair of mine," Star says, "and it doesn't matter anyway. I wasn't there at midnight."

Star convinces me.

Renée smiles. "We'll see about that. Have a nice day!" She and Ping turn and walk away. Pong and I follow.

"Wait a minute. What about my hat?" Star calls after her.

My hat? I think. Is she admitting guilt? I wonder.

"We're keeping it as evidence," Renée says.

The door slams.

"Have you ever heard the expression 'Keep your enemies close'?" I ask her.

"What do you mean?" Renée slows down.

"Keep moving," I tell her. "I don't want Mr. Rupert to catch us out here." We walk another block toward the Bennetts' house. "It means you want to know what your enemies are up to. Even if Star's behind the stolen fish and Grumpy, you should have been nicer to her."

"Oh, she's behind them, all right. I want to smoke her out."

As we draw nearer to the Bennetts' house, our search dogs droop again, slowing down. Ping actually plants his paws stubborn donkey–style and refuses to budge. Renée scoops him up and kisses him on the head. "I'm sorry, Poochy-cakes. We'll see you after school again."

We get them into the house. "Bye, Pong!" I pat the big dog and then fill up his water bowl.

Ping puts on his cuteness show complete with a perfect back-straight royal sit, then a paw shake and a roll over. Renée gives his belly a rub and he waves his front paws to tell her to keep going.

But then Beethoven's Fifth plays and she stops to answer her phone. "Hi, Reuven. What's up?" Her brows crease. "No, of course not. We borrowed your wagon yesterday and returned it in perfect condition." She shakes her head. "How would I know how it got dented?"

I mouth the word *Grumpy* at her.

She mutes the phone. "He's not grumpy, usually," she tells me. "He's just upset about a dent in his wagon." She turns her attention to her phone again and unmutes. "Fine. Goodbye."

"I meant those teens used Reuven's wagon to steal Grumpy last night!" I say.

Renée snaps her fingers. "We should call the cops. They could dust it for prints."

"Do you really think they'd bother for a garden gnome? Or even a bunch of wooden fish?"

"They should. It's art, and art is important to people."

"You're right. Mr. Rupert really wants his mailbox back." We leave the dogs and lock up the Bennetts' house. "But I don't even think the police will investigate." That thought becomes mistake number two of the day.

At that moment, a squad car passes us, slows down, and stops … where else but at my house.

Of course they're going to investigate; and they're going to start with us.

DAY TWO, MISTAKE THREE

"What are the police doing at my house?" My voice squeaks. I sound like a mouse and feel like one, too.

"Relax. We haven't done anything wrong," Renée soothes. "Don't act so nervous."

"I'm just going to tell them the truth." Despite her patting my back like I'm a puppy, I'm getting more anxious; my voice speeds up and goes higher. "I don't want to be caught with fish in my pants like last time."

"What are you talking about? You don't have any of the stolen fish in your pockets today, do you?"

"No. I mean that like a metaphor. You know, what Mrs. Worsley talked about in English class." I'm babbling now. "If we don't tell the police what we know right away, they'll find it all out later and blame us. It'll be like when they made me empty my pockets."

"Okay, okay. Let's stop for a moment. Take a breath."

She's right, maybe they'll just leave if we wait long enough. I inhale deeply and look up to the sky. As I exhale, something black sitting in a tree catches my eye. "Hey! Check it out. Red's been at it again."

"What are you talking about?"

"See, up there."

She looks up and shrugs.

"It's one of Red's dog-doo bags."

"That guy in grade eight?"

"Yeah, the one with red hair. When he walks his Pomeranian, he bags his poop and leaves it in trees to scoop later on his bike. 'Course then he forgets." I reach up and grab it. Dad insists we clean up after other dog owners so they don't close the streets or the park entirely to dog walkers.

"What are you going to do with that?" Renée asks.

"Put it in our garbage can."

"If stalling makes you feel better, go for it."

I shake my head. "It doesn't." I inhale again as we come closer to the squad car. "Do you think I can knit a couple of rows before we talk to the police?"

"Oh, probably. Did it ever occur to you that they maybe don't even want to talk to us at all? Maybe they're asking your dad if he noticed someone taking the Grumpy gnome from the Lebels' yard. Maybe they'll pull away before we go in."

I let my breath out. "You're right. I'm calmer now. We can keep going."

But the car does not leave before we make it to the driveway. The tinted, dark windows at the back of the squad car make it impossible to see inside. There's a picture of a dog's head on the side and the words *K-9 Unit* at the back. Up close, that police car makes my breath rush.

"Don't worry. Come on. Let's just go in and see what's up." Renée takes my hand now. If anyone were looking, this would be embarrassing. But for right now, it helps me. I open the door and step inside. So far, so good.

"Stephen, get in here!" my father calls. "The police need to ask you some questions."

So much for them not wanting to talk to us.

We step into the family room, and there, sitting on the couch sipping coffee, are Constable Jurgensen and Constable Wilson.

"Where's Troy?" Renée asks.

"He's in the car," Constable Jurgensen answers. "We understand Mrs. Noble has allergies."

"Don't worry, the car is climate controlled," Constable Wilson adds. "Troy's napping."

"Apparently, Mr. Rupert called the police to report two kids matching your description out at the park at one in the morning," Dad says.

"In their pajamas," Constable Wilson adds.

"Really? We weren't out at 1:00 a.m.," Renée protests. "I didn't even bring pajamas to the sleepover, remember? I wore Stephen's old sweatpants and a T-shirt to bed last night."

"At one in the morning, we were in bed," I say, certain we were back by then. We couldn't have been out there more than half an hour. The cellphone in my pants pocket vibrates. "Excuse me, may I go to the bathroom?"

"Sure," Constable Wilson says.

Constable Jurgensen, however, frowns. He stares after me as though I have something to hide.

And I do. I rest my hand on the top pocket of my cargos where my cellphone vibrates a second time. Probably nothing. Or maybe it's Mrs. Bennett telling me she's home from London and doesn't need me to walk Ping and Pong tonight. She's a flight attendant like mom, which is how we got her as a customer.

Or maybe the phone call is from a new client. We handed out flyers a few weeks ago with this number on it, after all. I give out our business cards all the time. This is an official Noble Dog Walking cellphone.

Still, adults expect you to ignore your phone when they're asking you questions. Right now, I need a break from Constables Jurgensen and Wilson. Maybe even some time to prepare.

I close the bathroom door behind me and raise the phone. Check the screen. It's a text:

Tell your little friend not to turn in my hat and hair to the cops. Or I go straight to Animal Control and show them what the dog did to my nose.

Just what I was afraid of — I can feel my heart turn into a giant turnip that pushes against my ribs and throat. The vines growing out of it are going to choke me. And, yes, that's a metaphor.

I type back: *You said you were asleep in bed last night. That's all I know.* Almost immediately, I feel my phone buzz again.

Good. Just keep it that way, Dog Boy.

Mistake number three of the day: misjudging Star. I really thought she was a nice person, someone who liked animals. Instead, she's ready to report Ping, which she must know could cost our Jack Russell client his life.

DAY TWO, MISTAKE FOUR

I head back to the family room, and this time, Renée asks to go to the bathroom. She has her hand on her pocket, too. Another phone call or text?

From the other pocket, that black knitted cap pokes out. How do I warn her not to give that hat to the police? That Ping's life could be at risk?

No chance. She's gone and Constable Jurgensen starts in on me right away.

"Why do you think Mr. Rupert would call us to report that you were in the park last night if you were asleep in your bed?"

I shrug my shoulders. "Mistaken identity? I know he doesn't like me because one of the dogs I walk pooped on his flowers."

"Did you clean it up?" Constable Jurgensen barks.

"Of course. He yelled at me as I was bagging it," I answer.

Constable Wilson shakes her head. "One of those." She sighs.

Constable Jurgensen squints at her for a moment, looking annoyed.

It occurs to me he may be "one of those" himself.

My father clears his throat for attention. "Stephen, if you can look me in the eyes and promise me that you were not outside at one in the morning, I will believe you, no matter what anyone else says."

I look him directly in the eyes. They're brown with crinkles around them. Teddy bear eyes, my mom says. You never lie to a teddy bear. But I do have a loophole here. Mr. Rupert exaggerated the time to the police, and like Renée said, she was never outside in pajamas. Not at any time.

"I promise, Dad." It's taking all my willpower not to break down and confess. But if we want to keep Ping safe, we certainly can't tell them what we saw now.

Renée returns, that black knitted cap hanging out even more, so it looks as though it may fall out any moment. Her hand still rests on the other pocket. "Me, too," she says. "I promise I wasn't out there at one, either."

"Well, that's good enough for me, officers," Dad says.

"Yes, we'll be going, then." Constable Jurgensen gets up.

"Say hi to Troy for us," Renée says.

"Hold up a second." Dad raises his pointer finger. "Let me give you one of my special treat bags for your dog." Constable Jurgensen's mouth opens, but before he can protest, Dad returns from the kitchen with a zip-lock bag of liver bites. "All hormone free," he says as he hands it to Constable Wilson.

"Thank you," she says.

"Yeah, thanks." Constable Jurgensen sounds more annoyed than grateful. He turns to Renée and me, points to his own eyes with two fingers, and says, "We'll be *seeing* you." He'll be watching us is what he's really saying. Then, as they head out the door, Constable Wilson stops and hands me her business card. "Call me if you think of anything else or see anything in the future."

We're all quiet for a few moments after they leave. It's like there's a big black hole between us and Dad. Then he turns to look our way, eyebrows raised like big, shaggy question marks.

"So what is that black thing hanging from your pocket?" Dad asks Renée.

"This?" she pulls it out. "Just a hat we found in the parking lot. We think we know who it belongs to so …"

Dad tilts his head. "Black hat. Doesn't everybody have one? I bought one at the dollar store myself."

"Yes, but nobody wears them till it's freezing out."

Dad nods. He has to assume it's something we picked up while walking the dogs just now since he believes us about not being out last night. But he's suspicious about something. "Well, your lunches are on the counter. Stephen, you changing out of your uniform?"

"Yeah, Dad."

"Better hurry up."

I nod and leave Renée gathering up her homework. In my room, I change into sweatpants and a sweatshirt 'cause on Fridays, it's gym. Never want to repeat my grade four boxers mistake, although Bruno and Tyson will never let me forget. At least I learn from my mistakes, I think, as I dash down the stairs and out the door with Renée.

A grey sky and some wind makes me hug my coat around me.

Renée hands me my lunch. Good thing, I nearly forgot. I stop to put it in my backpack. She starts walking again, only in the wrong direction.

I follow. "Where are we going?" I ask.

"Listen," she answers, "Attila called me before. I have to do something for him. It will probably make me really late for class."

"No, no, no, no! You can't be late." I shake my head, but keep walking alongside her, anyway. "Dad trusts us. Your parents will be mad at him!"

"You don't have to come if you don't want. But Attila's at Mr. Kowalski's house. And he needs a piece of art to submit to that contest you told me about."

"I don't get it. He's never all that nice to you."

"What are you talking about? We hang around together all the time."

"You're in the same house before and after school, sure; it's where you both live. But do you ever do anything together?"

"We used to draw …"

"Lately?" I ask.

"Well, sure. Just the other day, his friends came over and they chased me around with Nerf guns."

"Guns! You said he wasn't violent."

"NERF guns. The bullets don't hurt. I had a gun, too. It was fun. We all laughed."

A gang of teenagers shooting Nerf pellets at Renée? Sure, they laughed — but to me, it just sounds mean. Which is exactly what I expect from Attila.

"Why can't he get the art himself?"

"'Cause Dad's kicked him out of the house. That's why he's staying with his art mentor."

"So you're okay going by yourself?" I look at her and she nods. But I know she's not. She only helps me with the dogs all the time 'cause she hates being alone.

I stop and Renée walks on alone as if to prove it. Half a block she trudges and doesn't look back. But I can't stop watching her. Finally, I decide.

This should count as my fourth mistake of the day. But like I said, she helps me with the dogs.

"Fine, I'm coming with you anyway."

DAY TWO, MISTAKE FIVE

"Let's run so we're not so late," I suggest, breaking into what's more like a fast walk. As I mentioned before, running is something neither of us is that good at. Renée begins moving more quickly, and the wind pushes us along as if it wants us to hurry, too.

My hands feel empty, jogging these long blocks without any dogs' leashes in them. "Listen" — I huff my words between steps — "when I was in the bathroom, I read a text from Star."

Renée nods again. "I know. Star wants you to wait a couple of days before saying anything about Grumpy."

"What? No! That's not what she said at all." I slow down. "She threatened to report Ping to Animal Control if we give up the hat to the police."

Renée tilts her head. "Really?" She slows down, too.

"Yup. I went to the bathroom just so I could read her text."

"Told you she wasn't nice."

We walk for a bit. Then I wonder out loud, "Why should waiting a couple of days make any difference?"

She shrugs her shoulder. "I don't know. Maybe she's leaving the country. We can only hope."

"Do you think the Lebels even noticed that Grumpy is gone?" I ask her.

"Maybe not. The pool's been closed for a while, right?"

"Yup." I glance at my watch. First bell right now. "We should get going," I tell Renée and we jog for a bit again. "What about the mailbox? And the gun? Is Star involved in that, too?"

"Of course she is," Renée answers. "Attila wouldn't discuss it with me. But he doesn't seem very worried about the charges."

"Is he ever?"

"No. Mom and Dad sure are."

"Uh-huh." I gesture with my thumb to the right. "Should we turn down this street, to avoid Mr. Rupert's house?"

"No. That will take even longer. Let's just sprint."

"*Sprint?* Gah! All right." We start running again.

When we finally get there, Renée's driveway is empty. Both her parents must be at work; Attila could have easily picked up his own painting. Mr. Kowalski probably has a car, too, even though I've only ever seen him jogging everywhere. Bet he could have driven Attila.

"How are we going to carry Attila's art to Mr. Kowalski's house?" I ask, not wanting to repeat the wooden fish mistake. "I bet Reuven doesn't want anyone using his wagon anymore."

"No worries, it's on a memory stick. I just have to get it from his desk."

"Really? He couldn't have emailed it to the Art Gallery of Burlington?"

She shrugs. "Probably doesn't accept art by email." She unlocks the door and I follow her to Attila's basement room. I've seen it before but it's still awesome. A king-sized bed, made up neatly in bright-fuchsia sheets and a duvet, dominates the room. A huge Banksy print hangs over it. In the print, a maid holding a dustpan lifts a blanket covering to reveal a brick wall.

"Of all the posters he could hang, why that one?" I ask.

"Represents sweeping problems under the carpet," Renée answers. "My dad takes it personally." She walks to the desk in the corner, opens a drawer, and pulls something out. "Got it!" she says, and we head back up the stairs and out the door.

"Mr. Kowalski lives over there." She points to the end of the street where a strange square house towers over all the others. I've often wondered who lives there.

It has pale-blue siding and a bright-red door. At the top, there's a railing around the roof as though someone might use it as a balcony. It's not even that far. Attila could have jogged over to get his own memory stick.

Instead, we power walk again. Neither of us wants to know what Mrs. Worsley will say when we arrive at school in the middle of gym class. As we get closer to Mr. Kowalski's house, I see the same beat-up old white van that Reuven's dad was driving yesterday parked alongside the odd house. Does Mr. Jirad work for Mr. Kowalski? *Pay the Artist* the message on the dent reminds us. Do people forget to pay for art?

We continue up the walkway and Renée presses the doorbell.

It gongs like a church bell and a wrinkled, tanned face peeks out. "Oh, good. You made it." Mr. Kowalski opens the door instantly and sweeps his hand back. "Come in!"

We wipe our shoes on the hairy brown mat in front of the door, then step onto the dark wooden floor.

The hallway, which seems to take up the entire front part of the house, has a vaulted ceiling and a chandelier that looks like it came from the phantom's opera house. Paintings hang all the way up the wall to the ceiling. Great paintings with bright colours, different shapes, strange faces — I can't help staring.

Renée hands Mr. Kowalski the memory stick.

"Thank you." He shakes it like a pointer. "Don't like my students uploading to cloud storage. You can't trust corporations with art! Attila, your sister is here!" he calls.

Attila appears and actually smiles when Mr. Kowalski waves the memory stick. "Thanks," he says.

First time I've ever heard that word from his lips.

"We're taking this directly to the gallery," Mr. Kowalski says. "Should we drop you off at school?"

"Yes, please," Renée answers.

My parents tell me never to accept a ride from strangers and Mr. Kowalski sure acts bizarre sometimes. Plus his van looks like it's been through a battle. Still, we're late for school and nobody asked me.

Attila rides shotgun next to Mr. Kowalski.

Renée and I scramble through the side door of the van and find a seat in the back, which is full of art. We squeeze in with a couple of paintings between us. The one facing me is wrapped in clear bubble wrap so I can see the soft blue sky and snowy landscape. It reminds me of the rabbit and boy picture hanging in our guest bedroom.

"We have a painting of yours," I tell Mr. Kowalski.

"You don't say?" He beams into the rear-view mirror as he starts up the van. "If you don't mind me asking, what gallery did you purchase it from? I haven't had that many exhibitions lately."

I think carefully about my answer. He obviously thinks Dad bought it.

We're driving by Mr. Rupert's house and I duck without even thinking about it. Then I bob up again, embarrassed. Mr. Rupert's never going to look for us in this van, after all. "Um, well. My father picked it up …" I let the sentence hang. Maybe he doesn't have to know it was on the curb at junk pickup day. We turn onto Duncaster, heading toward our school.

Renée doesn't think as hard before finishing my sentence. "Someone left it on the curb near a recycling bin just over there, yesterday." She points. This counts as mistake five of the day. Or maybe the error was accepting the lift in the first place.

"What!?" Mr. Kowalski rises up out of the driver's seat and turns to the back, letting go of the wheel completely. The van hits the curb and bumps over it, two wheels on, two off.

A few hundred metres ahead, Madame X stands at the crosswalk watching. If she's anything like our previous crossing guard, Mr. Ron, she will want to report Mr. Kowalski's driving. That's if the van doesn't run her over first.

DAY TWO, MISTAKE SIX

Hitting the curb forces Mr. Kowalski to face the road again and pay attention to driving. He grabs the wheel and steers the van down onto the street again. *Clunk, clunk!* It rolls to a stop; he shuts off the engine and turns around again to face us. "Where exactly did you find my work?"

"Oh, you know. At that house with the crazy little dogs!" Renée answers.

"Jessica Irwin! That witch!" he cries. "She cheated on our bet."

"What bet?" Renée asks.

"She refused to insure the art in the staff room. Says no one wants to steal art."

"Didn't you redecorate the lounge in a lodge motif?" I am pretty sure that awful fish plaque doesn't need any insurance.

"Her idea again! Cost cuts, cost cuts. Then she left the original art in random places to prove no one would take it. We bet on it."

"My father didn't 'take' anything, just so you know," I tell him. "He rescued the painting — the garbage collectors would have trashed it."

His mouth drops. "She put it near the trash to devalue it."

"But he loves it!" Renée quickly adds. "We all do!"

I nod quickly.

Out of the corner of my eye, I spot Madame X marching toward us now. Left, right, left, right. She looks about ready to clobber Mr. Kowalski with her stop sign. When she gets to the van, she raps on the passenger window and Attila opens it.

"Everybody okay in here?" she asks. "Should I call medic?"

"No, we're all fine," Attila answers.

"You are parked in crossing zone. You should go now."

I undo my seat belt. "It's okay, we can get out here," I tell Mr. Kowalski. Renée and I scramble to climb out the side door. "When will the winners be announced?" I call back as we step up to the sidewalk.

"Five o'clock tomorrow," Attila answers. "There will be a reception. Why don't you and Renée come?"

Wow, he surprises me a second time today. "Okay, I'm sure my dad will come, too. Good luck, Attila," I say.

He smiles.

Then I pull a business card from my pocket and hand it to Mr. Kowalski. "If you want the painting back, you can just call me."

"Oh, no. Your father may have accidentally helped me with my bet. Can you just take a picture of it hanging on your wall?"

"Sure. Hope you win the bet," I say.

"Oh, I will. I still have a paintbrush or two up my sleeve." He winks at me and then they drive off.

Renée stares after the van, her eyebrows crushed together. She's thinking hard about something. "The paintbrush thing, that's a metaphor, right?"

"Who cares," I say. "Let's get to the office before the absentee line calls our parents."

We rush the rest of the way, but we're still twenty minutes late. What to say to the secretary, I wonder, as we make our way to the front counter.

But I don't have to worry; Renée takes over the talking. "I had to double back home to get my gym clothes," Renée tells her. "And my friend Stephen came with me so I wouldn't have to go alone."

Her friend. She makes me sound like a hero. I like it.

The secretary clicks her tongue but writes out our slips without even looking up. "Don't be late again or you'll get a week's detention."

"We won't," Renée promises, and then we take off out the door.

"Whoa, are we ever lucky," I tell her outside the office.

She nods. "And maybe, if we walk slowly, we won't have to play dodge ball."

"Good thinking." After all that rushing, it's nice to just stroll slowly toward the gym. On the way, we spot Mrs. Klein mopping the morning muck from the floor.

Renée waves hello and grins.

We're getting closer and she's opening her mouth to talk to her. Oh, no! "Whatever you do, don't ask her about Mr. Rupert," I warn her under my breath.

"Mrs. Klein, are you and Mr. Rupert going out?" she calls.

Oh, come on! You're not supposed to ask adults those kinds of questions. Even Renée should know that.

Mrs. Klein stops mopping and smiles. She once told me that no one notices the cleaning staff. "Yes, we are. Isn't it wonderful?" She sighs.

Maybe, in fact, she likes being asked.

"I never expected to find love again at my age."

"Wonderful," I repeat. The thought of her getting all kissy-faced with Mr. Rupert actually makes me want to hurl. I nudge Renée. "Maybe we can still make that dodge ball game, if we hurry."

But Renée can't be stopped. "How did you two meet?"

You would think at this point Mrs. Klein would ask us if we didn't have some place to go. That's sure what Mrs. Worsley would do.

Instead, her smile stretches wider. She sighs again. "One night I worked late all by myself and heard some noises."

Renée nods sympathetically. "I hate being alone."

"Since that car drove into the school, I've become very nervous. This time, I got so spooked I ran outside of the building. And there he was." She stops and smiles. "My hero."

Her hero? Or was he the one making the noises?

"Mr. Rupert?" Renée asks.

"Yes. He came inside with me and did a thorough inspection of the building. He didn't find anything, of course. But I felt so safe …"

"That was nice of him," I say, grabbing Renée's elbow and moving her along.

Mrs. Klein nods. "And we've been seeing each other ever since."

"Okay, well, later!" Renée says as I drag her farther away. Mrs. Klein starts mopping again.

Our little chat eats another five minutes of class.

Mrs. Worsley takes our late slips and frowns at us. "All right, you two. You need to warm up before starting in on the game. I want you to jog around the gym three times."

Gahhh! More running!

"Okay, Mrs. W." I take a deep breath and start.

"I'm just going to change first," Renée says as I start running.

Into what? I wonder. Whatever. She scores another five-minute delay and comes out in the sweats and T-shirt I loaned her last night. The pant legs pool up around her ankles. She won't be able to dodge anything if we make it into the game. But we don't want to, anyway. Tyson and Bruno can be brutal when they aim the ball at us.

I slow down to pace myself and Renée takes the lead. We have twenty-five minutes of gym left and we make sure the laps last right till the end.

The rest of the day feels like a walk in the park after our early morning workout. That's a simile not a metaphor.

On the way home, I just know what Renée will suggest, her brother not being at home for her at all. So mistake number six — I even know it as I make it — is asking her myself.

"It's not a school night. Do you want to sleep over again?"

DAY TWO, MISTAKE SEVEN

Renée nods like crazy. "Yes, please! A sleepover!"

"We're not going outside after dark, no matter what happens," I warn her.

"Of course not. I'm exhausted. After supper, I'm going straight to bed."

"Sure, you are. You know we still have to walk the dogs, right?"

"As long as we don't run. We can pick up some clothes for me on the way." Renée grins.

Oh, great, walking by Mr. Rupert's again.

When we arrive home, Dad proudly shows us his first complete dog sweater: tiny and sky blue with a stripe of orange and indigo around the neck and leg holes.

"That is a piece of art, Mr. Noble," Renée says.

"Wow, yeah," I agree. "Speaking of which, Dad, can we go to the Art Gallery of Burlington tomorrow? There's a special show opening."

He grins, still thinking about his masterpiece. "Sure. What time?"

"Five." I don't even know if he's listening. "And can Renée sleep over again?"

His head snaps up and he turns to her. "You know, you'll have to go home sometime. Your family is going to be working through Attila's, *um*, problem for a while."

"Maybe. But maybe not." Renée smiles. "I have a feeling we're going to be able to clear his name really soon."

How does she expect to do that when he's on a surveillance tape holding stolen goods? Renée must have some ideas, and I'm dying to find out what they are. Something tells me it would be a mistake to discuss these around Dad, though.

"Fine. Let your mom and dad know, though," Dad reminds her.

"Great!" I change the subject. "Let's grab a snack." I tip my head toward the kitchen and give Renée the eye.

"I bought honeycrisp apples for you." Dad picks up his knitting needles; there's red wool on them this time.

"Thanks." The two of us head for the kitchen. "Peanut butter or chocolate spread on your apple?"

"Chocolate," Renée answers.

I put a few tablespoonfuls in a cup and stick it in the microwave. As the chocolate melts, I chop up a couple of apples. "So what do you know that I don't?"

"Nothing. But I have a plan."

"What is it?" The microwave beeps.

"It came to me when you asked your dad about the art show. We have to make sure all our suspects go to the show."

"How?"

Dad strolls in at that moment and I close my mouth. It's too obvious we've stopped talking because of him.

"Try one," I quickly offer, holding out the plate of apple slices to him.

"Uh-huh." He takes an apple slice and dips, still squinting at me. "You know, I believed you about not going out last night." He bites into the apple and chews a while as I feel guilt spread warm across my face. "Mmm, that is so good." He licks his fingers.

The phone rings. "That will be your mother," Dad says. "Why don't you pick up?"

Yay! I can't help smiling as I grab the receiver. "Hello?"

"Hi, Stephen. How are you?"

I can hear the hug in her voice. "I'm good, Mom." And at that moment, I am so good. "I miss you."

"Me, too. I'll be home tomorrow."

"We're going to an art gala at five. Will you be back in time?"

"No. I'll be home around seven."

"Oh." I breathe through my disappointment for a couple of moments, then change the subject. "Remember yesterday, how you said Mr. Rupert has never been the same since his wife died? What did you mean? Is he dangerous?"

"Oh, I don't know. He's very angry at the world. Stephen, please don't worry about him." She pauses for a moment, then changes the subject. "You'll never guess what flew on the plane today."

"You don't sound stuffed up, so not a cat or a dog, right?" Mom's allergies usually give her a runny nose and eyes.

"Not a cat or dog, that's right. It was … a turkey!"

"You mean for dinner … or in cargo?"

"No, neither. Right in the passenger cabin. Know how our airline allows service animals?"

"Yeah, but what can a turkey do? Guide a blind person?"

My mom chuckles.

"Or is it a hearing ear turkey?" We both laugh.

"He provides therapy," Mom finally answers.

"Say what?"

"The passenger carried a psychiatrist's note that said the turkey calms him. That it was his companion turkey. So we had to let him board, no extra charge."

"A companion turkey. Maybe I need one of those."

"Oh, Stephen. I'll be home soon. I miss you." I can hear her smile across the miles. "Listen, I have to board now. Love you."

"I love you, too, Mom."

"Bye."

I hang up and face Dad again. "She had to go."

He nods. "Back to what I was saying before. If you tell me something, I will believe you. But … I don't want you two hunting around the neighbourhood for some crazy gunman at any time of day." He knows something; he must. Or he heard us.

"No hunting," Renée promises with a chocolatey grin.

"No hunting," I agree, making a tiny cross over where I think my heart is. That's where it's doing a little backflip right now, anyway, 'cause mistake number seven of the day is that we're doing something even more dangerous. We're *inviting* a gunman to an art show.

DAY TWO, MISTAKE EIGHT

After we're finished snacking, Renée sits down across from Dad in the family room and picks up her knitting.

"Guess I'll go change," I tell them and climb the stairs to my bedroom. Sniffing my Noble Dog Walking shirt for B.O., I decide it's still fresh enough. I only wear it a couple of hours a day. My cargo pants have a fleck of what could be ketchup on the top pocket. I scrub that off with a washcloth. I want to wear my official uniform. It makes me professional.

When I get back down, Dad's showing Renée how to change colours on her scarf. It's already a foot long. "If you're going to keep walking the dogs with Stephen, we should get you a uniform, too," Dad says.

"Really?" she squeals. "I would love that!"

Of course she would.

Dad must really like Renée: the uniforms cost money and he is really cheap. If she becomes official, I'll have to split my pay with her, too.

With a big grin on her face, she keeps knitting, fast and smooth. "I love this red!" The stitches on her scarf look nice and even, not tight and scrunchy like mine. Miss Perfect. I'll never catch up.

I grab our jackets from the closet and throw Renée hers. "Come on, let's go!"

"See you later," she tells Dad.

"Bye," I call and we head out the door to the Bennetts'. By now I'm really regretting inviting Renée to another sleepover. I don't feel sorry for her at all. I'm feeling mean, and before I can help myself, the meanness spills out in words. "So if your brother gets convicted, are you going to want to move into our house?"

Her mouth drops open; her eyes moonsize. "He's. Not. Guilty."

And in that moment, I realize something. Despite what she keeps saying, she's not really sure at all; she just keeps hoping.

"Okay," I say gently as we walk. "So how are you going to get all our suspects to the show?"

"We'll invite them now on our way with the dogs."

"All of them? They may not come," I say.

"Sure, they will, if I tell them I'm going to announce the name of the criminal."

"If you do that, Star will report Ping to Animal Control."

"She's already going to the art opening with Attila. We won't tell her."

"I thought she was his ex-girlfriend."

Renée's mouth bunches up. "She likes to dangle him from her finger." She turns her own pointer finger into a hook. "Like a fish."

We reach the Bennetts' now. Best part of the day. Pong waits calmly at the window, paws leaning on the glass, black eyes watching for us, his long tail waving in the background. Ping's already bouncing up and down, barking a hysterical welcome.

Then, when we get in, there's wagging and licking. It's hard to calm them down enough to snap the leashes on.

Pong pulls me out the door and Ping pushes at my legs to get ahead. "So, do we really have to ask Mr. Rupert?"

"No. If we can catch Mrs. Klein at school, we'll suggest she come and tell her to bring him." Renée allows Ping the lead and he proudly struts forward.

"Brilliant. Let's swing that way first." Pong salutes a hydrant, which reminds me of the recycling bins yesterday and the painting left on the curb at Mrs. Irwin's house. "What about inviting Dad's Yorkie client?"

"You're right. She's definitely suspicious. Pretty sure the dogs picked up those stolen fish at her recycling bin."

We're closing in on her house. Our wagon team wants to drag us there anyway because the Yorkies are yapping from behind the gate. Good thing they're in the backyard. It means Ping and Pong can't scrap with them at the front door.

"Well, will you look at that!" Renée suddenly says to me.

I don't know what she's talking about so she shoves me and points.

Even the dogs pause for a moment and train their eyes on the school parking lot, wagging expectantly.

First I spot the bright-green Cadillac with the "Support Our Troops" bumper sticker. Then I see our custodian, Mrs. Klein, walking toward it with Mr. Rupert. But she looks taller than usual, her red hair poofier. Are those high heels on her feet? Yes, snazzy tall boots, and she's definitely wearing lipstick.

Mr. Rupert's lightning-rod hair looks calmed down. He's wearing a blue camel coat over dress pants, a pale mauve shirt, and darker violet tie.

"Mr. Rupert is smiling!" Renée comments.

"And all dressed up!"

"Oh, Mrs. Klein!" Renée waves. Ping barks, which really attracts Mr. Rupert's attention.

"Stop that! What are you doing?" I knock her hand down.

"I'm inviting her to the gallery, like I said." Renée gives a smarmy grin. "Don't they look cute together?" She crosses the street with Ping.

Pong and I follow reluctantly.

Mrs. Klein turns toward us, smiling. "Hi there!"

Mr. Rupert scowls.

"Would you like to attend the Art Gallery of Burlington reception tomorrow?" Renée calls out. "It's at five o'clock. Free to the general public."

"Why, how nice of you to think of me," she says. "No one at school ever asks me to anything."

"Yes and you can bring Mr. Rupert," I quickly add. His scowl twists. I cross my fingers behind my back. "I mean, we'd really like it if he came."

If he has a gun on him, he'll pull it out and shoot me now.

"That's so thoughtful! Tom, wouldn't that be lovely? You like art, don't you?"

Tom, I think. Not grouch, but Tom. Of course, we haven't been thoughtful at all. We just want to find our thief and gunman, to clear Attila's name.

He shrugs his shoulder, growls, and nods.

"I think a trip to an art gallery would be wonderful," Mrs. Klein beams. "Thank you. We will definitely be there. Do you need a lift?"

Renée's eyebrows leap up.

"No, no!" we both answer.

"My father will drive us," I say.

"Well, we'll see you there, then." She smiles and walks off.

Mr. Rupert rushes around his big green car and opens the passenger door for her. "Wow," Renée says. "He's being nice to someone."

The car careens out of the lot and drives past us. Mrs. Klein smiles at us. Mr. Rupert doesn't look our way. Good thing, too; we didn't want him running us over on the sidewalk. We cross back over to Mrs. Irwin's side of the street.

The Yorkies' barking reaches orchestra level as we walk to the door.

Renée rings the doorbell, which sounds more like a buzzer.

No one answers, but we know Mrs. Irwin must be home or the dogs wouldn't be outside. I hit the doorbell now. At the side, the Yorkies begin tumbling over each other.

Mrs. Irwin finally wrenches open the door. She's dressed all in black except for a rainbow-coloured scarf loosely knotted around her neck. One hand reaches up to her hair as though she needs to hold it up. She seems put out by our visit.

"Hi, there," Renée says, smiling. "We want to make sure you know about the reception at the Burlington Art Gallery tomorrow at five o'clock. The winner of the art show will be announced."

Raff, raff, raff! The Yorkies clearly want to come.

"Quiet, Rosie!" Mrs. Irwin calls. "They're sending children out to canvas? How desperate can they get."

"Oh, nobody sent us."

Raff, raff, raff! More Yorkie yapping. "Shut up, Blue!" Mrs. Irwin calls.

How does she know which one it is? "I'm with Noble Dog Walking." I talk over the noise. "My dad walks your dogs."

Ping growls to answer the Yorkies.

Mrs. Irwin's eyes do a little roll. "Absolutely no one cares enough to come to the art show. I can leave art anywhere and it's safe."

She's definitely going to be our tough sell.

"Just to let you know, my father picked up that painting you left on the curb."

"Really, the painting with the rabbit and the snow?"

"We love it. I can get a photo of it hanging on our wall, if you like."

"True," Renée agrees. "We walk dogs, too. Obviously." She motions to Ping, who leaps at Mrs. Irwin's leg now. One of Mrs. Irwin's eyebrows reaches up high as she blocks Ping with her hands.

Renée yanks on the leash to get him down, then scoops him up. He licks her face as she talks. "We're able to see a lot of what goes on in the neighbourhood." More barking interrupts her. Renée closes her fingers around Ping's snout and raises her voice. "And we've noticed lots of art disappearing."

Mrs. Irwin's other eyebrow shoots up and her mouth puckers. That's when Renée launches mistake eight of the day. She could be warning our criminal.

"Tomorrow at the reception, we will be announcing who's been stealing it."

DAY TWO, MISTAKE NINE

Mrs. Irwin's cheeks turn red. She looks furious. "Nobody steals art!"

Her bluster makes me wonder just how much money she bet Mr. Kowalski.

"Well, that's not true," Renée answers. "Someone took Mr. Rupert's mailbox."

One of the Yorkies growls now. Another one yips. "Quiet, Hunter!" Mrs. Irwin calls to the dogs. "A mailbox?" she repeats.

"His wife made it," I explain. "My dad says her mailboxes were works of art."

"Someone stole all our hand-painted fish from the Stream of Dreams project at our school," Renée says.

"A sculpture disappeared from our neighbour's backyard." I don't tell her it's one of the seven dwarves. "And somebody made off with Mrs. Whittingham's Halloween display."

"Really? Perhaps we should define art. Somebody made off with my recycling bin last month. Does that count as stealing art, too?"

"No. It's just a thing people use."

"You see, you've just put your hammer on the nail. Art is useless!"

"No, it's not!" I argue. I think about that painting of the rabbit and the boy. The sleepy whiteness of the snow against the pale blue, the way it makes me feel all calm. "Art does something for me … inside."

Mrs. Irwin waves her hand, as if that doesn't matter. "I *am* coming to the gallery tomorrow. I'm afraid I have to. I'm a judge."

"You're kidding," I say.

At this point, the Yorkies at the side of the house turn psycho, snarling, hissing, yipping, and barking.

Mrs. Irwin's eyes bug out of her head. "I — told — you — all — to — SHUT UP!" She yells the last words. Then she dashes inside the house and slams the door.

Renée and I stare at the closed door for a moment, then turn to each other.

"Well, she's a bit high-strung, isn't she?" Renée finally says.

I shrug my shoulders. "An artist."

"An artist who doesn't value art." Renée sighs.

"Imagine working at something you don't even think is important. It would make you angry."

"Enough to carry a gun?" Renée wonders out loud.

"She wouldn't have stolen it from Mr. Rupert's house, though, would she?" I say.

A voice shrieks from the side of the house now. "Get in the house! All of you, Rose, Hunter, Blue, Violet, Goldie!"

Renée's eyes pop and she shakes her head. "Anything is possible."

"C'mon, we have other people to talk to."

Down the street, I spot our crossing guard leaving her post a little late today. "Boy, Madame X sure seems dedicated."

"Mr. Ron always worked late, too," Renée says, defending our last crossing guard. "Look, she's wearing that bulky coat again when it's not even cold yet."

"Doggies!" Mrs. Filipowicz calls. "Visiting school too late. All finished for today." She chuckles and then drops down to pat them. Ping jumps on her; Pong slaps her with his tail.

"Would you like to come to the award show at the Art Gallery of Burlington tomorrow?" Renée asks. "Five o'clock. I hear there will be refreshments."

"Oh, yes. I em coming. I entered!"

"You're an artist?" I ask.

"Back home I em, how do you say, *pisanka* master. For contest, I paint special egg in honour of my new home."

"Are you cold?" Renée asks. I elbow her.

"No, I em wearing lovely warm coat. A gift. Do you see?" She throws her shoulders back and points to it with her stop sign and other hand.

"Aren't you too hot in it, though?" Renée just cannot be stopped.

"Sometimes. Better to be too warm than cold, yes? And I need all the pockets."

The pockets!

She pats them. "I keep snacks and bandages. Water bottle. Sunscreen. Chapstick. Cell. Screwdriver."

Stolen fish. Only I know 250 fish won't fit in them, and they're too heavy for one person to carry. We could barely haul them on Reuven's wagon, yesterday.

"A screwdriver?" Renée repeats.

"Is multi-purpose." She pulls it from her pocket to show us. It's black and red and looks like a small torpedo. "Seven heads. Only screwdriver I will ever need."

"What do you even need a screwdriver for?" Renée asks. "I mean, on the job."

"You never know." Madame X flips a switch. "Also acts as flashlight!" A thin beam shines from it. She smiles.

"Nice!" I tug at Renée.

"Bye, Mrs. Filipowicz," we both say at the same time.

"I think that's everybody," Renée says proudly. "Not so hard at all."

"Not nearly everybody. Our thief could be anyone. Someone we don't even know. With no motive at all."

"Well, is there anyone else you'd like to see at the event?" Renée asks.

My mother; my best friend, Jessie, whom I haven't seen since the summer he moved away. Renée's parents maybe. "You know, I think everyone should come out to look at Burlington's art entries."

Renée nods. Her eyes sparkle and her eyebrows do a two-step shuffle. "People sometimes just need a push." She smiles as though she knows so much more than I do. "We should invite everyone we see."

The dogs give us their usual tug and run through Brant Hills Park. When we spot Mrs. Ron enjoying a cigar outside on her patio, we steer them that way and invite her to the gallery.

"Yup, yup, yup. Goin' already. My Ronnie's friend entered. Made one of them inukshuks out of brick."

"Mason man did?"

She nods. "Not just any brick. Antique. From a farmhouse."

"Cool," Renée says.

"See you, then." We cross the park back to the road. The dogs slow down as we hit the sidewalk again.

As we head to Renée's, we pass Mrs. Whittingham's house, and I blush remembering how I picked up what I thought was a dead baby. "I'm going to invite Mrs. Whittingham. If we catch the crook, she'll find out what happened to her Halloween display."

I ring the doorbell and a droolly little kid in diapers opens the door. "Get Mommy," I tell him.

He sticks his thumb in his mouth and just stares at me.

Mrs. Whittingham suddenly appears anyway, pushing her hair out of her eyes.

Renée takes over. "Hi. Did you know that to-morrow they're announcing the winners of the Burlington Art Show at the gallery at five o'clock?"

"I may have known that. August here goes to fingerpainting class after his nap. We'll stay for the announcement, for sure. Thanks for telling us."

"My brother entered. He's very good," Renée says proudly.

"Yeah! I saw his tank graffiti in the paper," Mrs. Whittingham says. "I thought it was explosive!"

Renée shrinks at the word. She really doesn't want the criminal to be Attila, and for her sake, neither do I.

Right next door to Renée's is Reuven's house.

"We have to invite him to come," I tell Renée.

"No, we don't. Look at his wagon." The bottom sags exactly where Grumpy rode. "We're the last ones he knows who borrowed it, too."

"Still. Did I tell you I saw Mr. Jirad driving Kowalski's van the other day?"

"Reuven's dad? No, you didn't."

"Well, I did. Anyway, we delivered Reuven's papers for him. He's got to let the wagon thing go in case he needs us again."

That kind of thinking becomes mistake number nine of the day. Or maybe it's just ever doubting Renée is right about anything. Still only nine mistakes today, I'm on a roll!

Pong and I scoot up Reuven's walk and ring the doorbell before Renée can stop us. Reuven answers the door immediately.

He shakes his finger at Renée behind me. "You owe me for my wagon!"

Ping barks himself hoarse, defending Renée against Reuven. Good that she holds his leash tight.

"My newspapers sink in the middle. The bottom's going to fall out any day," Reuven says over the barking.

"We left your wagon in perfect condition," I tell him. "Sit, Pong! Shh!" The dog grumble-growls a little and then does as he's told.

"Oh yeah? Then who dented it like that?"

"You'll find out if you come to the Art Gallery of Burlington tomorrow," Renée starts. "They're announcing —"

Ping leaps up suddenly and twists, yanking Renée around with him. He barks in a different, higher-pitched tone. More frantic.

Pong pulls me backwards, too, and I see, over on the sidewalk behind us, Star standing and listening to our conversation.

"Dad asked me to go to the opening tomorrow," Reuven tells us over Ping's noise. "We're helping Mr. Kowalski set up."

I fold my arms across my chest and stare at Star. She forms a pretend gun with her hand and shoots at Ping. Then she strolls on. I can feel my face heat up.

Renée rolls her eyes, then continues the conversation as though nothing has happened. "So your father's interested in art?"

"More gardening art. He loves topiary. Going to start teaching it at the Royal Botanical Gardens."

"What's topiary?" I ask.

"Sort of like sculpting only with trees and bushes."

"Cool," Renée says. "Well, I guess we'll see you there, then."

"About my wagon …"

"Don't worry! If we can't find the real vandal," she says, "we'll pay for a new one out of our dog-walking money."

Say what?

She and Ping lead the way to her house now.

"I can't believe you promised him that," I complain as she unlocks the door.

"We saw those ninja teens with Reuven's wagon. We know one of them is Star." She steps into the house with Ping and Pong and I follow.

"C'mon. Do you want her to report Ping to Animal Control?"

"She's not going to do that. Not if we can get her to confess on her own."

"Did you not see what she did back there?"

"Yeah. She messed with your head. Here, take Ping."

I take his leash in the same hand as Pong's and he circles me.

"I'll run upstairs and get some clothes."

"Okay." Ping circles me again, tightening the leash around me, tying up my legs. Pong sits down quietly and lets go a long whine.

day three

THE GREAT MISTAKE

MYSTERIES

DAY THREE, MISTAKE ONE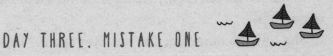

Later that night, even though she promised we wouldn't go out and she would go directly to bed, Renée wakes me and drags me to the window of the guest bedroom. "Do you see him?" Renée asks me.

It's past midnight, and I stand blinking sleep from my eyes. Her pajamas have spotted Dalmatians with sequined collars on them. They're blinding me.

"Here, take these. I brought them from home just in case." Renée hands me a small set of binoculars.

Squinting through the lenses, I sweep the school parking lot and then back again. "No, I do not see him. And no matter what, we are not going outside." One more sweep of the schoolyard produces a shadow. I swing the binoculars back. "Oh, wait a minute. Who's that? It's Mr. Rupert! He's wearing camouflage fatigues!"

"What's he doing? Breaking into the school?"

"No, no. He's sneaking around the corner."

"Let me see!" She snatches back the binoculars and holds them up to her eyes. "Looks like he's hunting for someone."

"Does he have a gun?" I ask.

"Not that I can see." She watches awhile. Then drops the binoculars. "Maybe we should call the police on him for a change."

"What do we tell them? He hasn't done anything wrong, yet."

She lifts the binoculars to her eyes again. "He's looking in the classroom windows. Oh. I guess there's no point in calling anymore. He's leaving."

"I guess not. Okay, well good night. Sleep tight."

"Wait! I can't just fall asleep instantly after that. Do you think you could read me some of *The Night Gardener*?"

I sigh, get the book, and while she lies back in the bed knitting, I read. By the time I'm halfway through the chapter, I hear her soft snores, so I take the needles from her hands and place her knitting project on the bureau next to her bed. Then I tiptoe back to my own room and lie down on my bed. Eyes wide open. Brain spinning about the story we're reading where this evil tree gives you your secret desire, all the while sucking out your health and soul. Mixed up in there, too, are thoughts about a loud, angry man in camouflage yelling over a missing mailbox; Reuven crabbing at Renée about his wagon; a woman screaming at her squirming, yapping pile of dogs; and a hundred-year-old jogger crashing a van with all of us in it.

The loud, angry man turns into a Grumpy sculpture; Reuven morphs into a dead baby in a swing.

There's a witch with a diamond in her nose, a black knitted cap on her head, a black turtleneck sweater, and crazy flowered leggings. "I'll get you and your little dog, too!" Wicked Witch of the West from *Wizard of Oz*. Why is Star talking like her?

"Never, never!" I repeat. This marks the first mistake of the day. Denial. Believing that this young witch has no power over my small, furry walking companion.

Out from behind the witch, our crossing guard pops, grinning. Madame X aims a screwdriver at me but it turns into a gun. "Art-ee-fish-ful," she says and fires.

That's when I sit up, wide awake, and realize it's morning. I've been having nightmares.

I try to shake the sleep off. It's Saturday today, and still early, but I hear the murmur of voices below, one female. Not Renée's. Mom's? No. It can't be, not yet. Later tonight, she'll arrive.

"Stephen?" Dad calls up. "Are you awake?"

"Just barely," I grumble but suspect he doesn't hear me.

"Could you come down? There's someone here to see you."

"Give me a minute," I holler. Then quick as I can, I throw on some clothes, go to the bathroom, and splash water on my face. As I brush my teeth, I look out the window and nearly choke.

Parked in our driveway is a white truck. The words on the side read "City of Burlington, Animal Control."

DAY THREE, MISTAKE TWO

Hand on the bannister, I'm ready to take the first step down the stairs when my knees begin to shake. I close my eyes, feeling everything turn liquid inside me. *Poor Ping!* The friendliest dog I know will be labelled a dangerous dog all because he likes to lick a little too enthusiastically. In my mind, I hear the Wicked Witch of the West: "I'll get you and your little dog, too." No, no, no! Someone shakes my shoulders. I open my eyes again and see Renée. "Stephen, what's wrong with you?"

"Star called Animal Control on Ping. Someone's downstairs waiting to talk to me."

"Okay, okay. Don't panic!" Renée keeps shaking me, her eyes moonsized. She seems pretty panicked herself. "It's her word against ours and we deny everything."

I nod and peel her hands from my shoulders. "Hurry. Get dressed and come down with me."

As I sit on the stairs waiting for Renée to change, the sweet vanilla smell of Saturday waffles calls up to me. Even as I continue to worry about Ping, my mouth waters. When Renée reappears, she's dressed like some kind of ballet princess with a red tutu, a sparkling red-and-black top, white tights, and glossy back dance slippers.

I can't help staring.

"What?" she asks.

"You look like you're performing in a show."

"Bright colours and sparkles give me power." She makes fists. "I like to wear them when I'm feeling a little nervous."

But she wears them all the time.

"Okay. Let's go, then." We scramble down the stairs together.

A muscular lady with curly, golden hair and a dark uniform sits on Dad's recliner in the living room, studying her clipboard.

"Grab a seat, kids." Dad slaps the empty couch next to him. "This is Ms. Lacey from Animal Control." He points to the lady across from him. "She received a complaint from one of our neighbours."

"We control the dogs very well," Renée says as we sit beside Dad. "It's not our fault when someone approaches the animals …"

I kick Renée's ankle to shut her up a second too late.

"What?" Dad says.

Ms. Lacey looks, jabbing her pointer finger on her clipboard. "The complaint states that you put your dogs' poop bags in the trees."

"What?" I sputter. "That's ridiculous."

"He's never done that," Renée agrees.

"Your neighbour sent us a photo." Ms. Lacey passes us a paper black-and-white copy of a shot of me reaching up into a tree where there's a small black bag. Ping and Pong stand at my feet.

"But I'm not putting that bag there. I'm taking it down. Dad insists we clean up after other dog owners. It's good public relations."

"Really?" The woman's voice smiles. "That's admirable." She pulls back the photo and tilts her head as she looks at it this time. "Hard to tell, though. You could be doing either."

"*I* know what I was doing," I tell her.

"Can you tell us who filed the complaint?" Dad asks.

"No. You are not actually being charged today. We're just letting you know about the complaint, delivering a warning, so to speak."

A warning. From Star. She's serious about this.

"Of course, if we get another complaint about you, we will look at pressing charges."

"I always dispose of dog doo properly," I tell her. "I bag it and chuck it. I don't decorate trees. That's a promise."

Ms. Lacey stands up. "Well, thank you for your time." Ms. Lacey's arm muscles flex as she shrugs into the navy blue jacket draped on the chair behind her. "If you do find out who puts the bags in the trees, let us know and we will pay them a visit."

Red, from grade eight, of course.

"We'll let you know," Renée lies brightly.

"All right. Bye, then!" Dad leads her back to the front door and Ms. Lacey leaves the house. We watch as she climbs into her truck and pulls out of the driveway.

"You two sure are attracting a lot of attention these days," Dad says. His eyebrows reach up as he takes his first good look at Renée. "Nice outfit, by the way ... You've dressed up a little early for the gallery show, though. You don't want to get syrup on your party dress."

"What do you mean, Mr. Noble? These are my everyday regular clothes."

"Never mind, then. Waffles are warming in the oven. Let's eat."

We follow Dad into the kitchen and help him set the table for breakfast. Renée wants chocolate hazelnut spread on her waffle. As we each grab our plates, the phone rings. Dad and I turn to look at each other. Not that many people call us on our land line.

"Your mother's not scheduled to call," Dad says, as he stands and picks up. "Oh, hi, honey, nice surprise." He shrugs his shoulders. "Sure. He's standing right here." He hands me our portable.

"Hi, Mom," I say.

"Hey, Stephen. I just had to call. Heard the strangest thing," she says.

"I have something really strange to tell you, too." As I speak, I watch Renée spread chocolate on each individual square of her waffle.

"You first, then."

I wasn't really sure I wanted to go first, though. "You know how you were saying Mr. Rupert was angry at the world because he lost his wife?" Renée looks up at me as she drizzles syrup over the chocolate.

"I hope you weren't worrying about that all this time."

"Well, maybe just a little. Anyhow, now he's dating our custodian."

"What? Really? Well, that's good. He needs someone in his life."

"They don't seem at all alike." I notice Renée closing her eyes as she enjoys another square of her breakfast.

"Well, they don't have to be. Remember the man who needed a companion turkey on my last flight?"

I chuckle. "Mrs. Klein is a companion turkey?"

Renée grins with chocolatey teeth now.

"No, I didn't mean that at all."

"It's a great metaphor," I tell her and explain what Mrs. Worsley taught us about comparing two unlike things.

Mom giggles, and hearing her makes me feel so much better. Seeing Renée's chocolatey teeth makes me laugh, too. She can be a bit of a turkey, for sure. Maybe she's my companion turkey now that Jessie's gone.

"What's your funny story?" I ask Mom finally.

"Well, you know how Mr. Bennett is a pilot and he's doing a Seattle to Beijing flight, right?"

"No. I only know he's away 'cause we're walking Ping and Pong so much …"

"Well, anyway. I saw him at the airport. He told me U.S. customs caught a Canadian with fifty-one turtles strapped to his legs just before the flight."

If I estimate the way Mrs. Worsley taught us by dropping the one and multiplying by four, that makes two hundred little green feet clawing at his legs the whole time. I feel them myself and scratch at my own legs. "Under his pants?"

"Yup. Wore sweats but they looked bulky, which is what made the customs guy pull him aside."

"Why would anyone do that to turtles?" I ask.

"Well, he said was smuggling them to pay for his education. He's an engineering student at Waterloo."

I cringe. The poor turtles. "Do people grind up their shells for medicine or something?"

"Nope. They just like them as pets."

"Well, that's good at least."

"Perfectly legal to buy them but you need special paperwork to export them. Nobody wants to spread disease."

"Fifty-one turtles," I repeat. Two hundred and fifty wooden fish, I think. Bulky sweatpants. That story makes me believe Madame X could be our art thief, with her heavy multi-pocketed coat. Maybe somehow in cahoots with Star?

"So I'll see you later tonight. Love you."

"Love you too, Mom." We hang up at the same time.

"Tell us about the turtles," Renée says.

As I load my waffles with strawberry jam, I repeat Mom's turtle-smuggling story.

Afterwards, when we head for the Bennetts', I panic again about Star calling Animal Control. "What are we going to do? If she reports Ping for biting her nose, he's sunk."

Renée stops walking and holds out her hand. "Give me your phone. Let me settle this once and for all!"

Renée's always right, isn't she? It should be a no-brainer to turn over my cell to her.

She wiggles her fingers, beckoning, insisting. "Come on, hurry up."

Dad says you should always listen to your inner voice. Mistake two of the day is ignoring it and turning over my cell.

DAY THREE, MISTAKE THREE

"What are you going to do with it?"

"I'm going to reply to Star." Renée's eyebrows knit as she keys in her message and reads it aloud: "*Thanks for sending Animal Control. The officers liked how well Ping behaved. We showed them his cut tongue. And ... send!*"

"But that's not true! Ping wasn't even here," I say.

With one fist digging in her hip, she squints at me as she hands back my phone.

"And you never put a poop bag in a tree, either," she answers.

"True. But your text may just make Star madder."

Renée shrugs. "Or maybe it will show her we're not so easily scared off."

We begin walking again until my cell buzzes. Our footsteps stutter to a stop as I read out loud: "*I've kept this picture to show Animal Control. Just in case.*"

I show Renée the gross selfie that comes with the text. It shows a large blister around Star's nose piercing.

"Oh *pu*-lease. A keloid. She gets those every other week. How can she prove it's the dog? There are no teeth marks."

Renée does not convince me. "All she has to do is press charges. I don't think she has to prove Ping guilty beyond reasonable doubt."

We arrive at the Bennetts' now and the dogs leap up in front of the window. *Sproingy, sproingy.* Ping's joy especially makes me grind my teeth over Star. He's such a funny dog. Makes everyone laugh except her.

"You're waving at them, you know," Renée says.

"So are you," I answer and grin. I unlock the door and Ping bounces from his back legs: up, down, up, down.

Renée scoops him into her arms and cuddles him. Little dogs hate that, which makes it a great way to calm Ping down.

Pong leans his body against mine, owning me with his big brown eyes. We leash them up quickly and I herd Pong through the door.

At the sidewalk, Renée sets Ping down. "There's an important piece of information that came of that Animal Control visit." Ping drags her forward.

"Really? What?"

Pong raises his leg against a lamppost.

"You can't tell from a picture whether a person is taking something or putting it back."

Ping salutes the post, too.

"I was taking the bag away." I reach for a dog bag in my pocket as Pong squats.

"Yes. I know that. But what if the opposite were true for Mr. Rupert's mailbox. What if Attila was returning the mailbox? Stupid Star probably stole it.

Which is why he isn't saying anything to the cops. He's protecting her."

I bend down to scoop Pong's poop now. "Why would she want to steal the mailbox someone's dead wife made?"

"She's a witch, okay?"

Renée has a point. "'I'll get you and your little dog, too,'" I repeat. "You know I dreamt about her." I stand up with the poop bag in my hand and twist a knot at the top. Star reported me for not disposing of my bags properly. Plus, after patting and allowing an innocent animal to lick her face, she threatens to report his only mistake, which was to love her too much. She is pure evil.

We stroll forward, Pong pulling into the lead. "Star's guilty of stealing Grumpy, no question. But remember my mom's phone call?" Ping nips at Pong's feet now. "The story about the bulky sweat-pants hiding the turtles? Kind of planted an idea in my head, too. I'm positive Madame X stole the fish using that big winter coat. She carries the multi-tool in her pocket, after all. I think she's the one who dumped them in the recycling across the street."

"Stop that, Ping." Renée holds him back from Pong's paws. "Why, though? And when would she have time?"

"After dark. She wouldn't take all of them at once. And who knows, maybe she had help."

"And she thought they were …" Renée forms air quotes with her fingers "'Art-ee-fish-ful.'"

"Plus, she told the cops we took them. She had to have noticed the fish in our wagon were blanks."

The dogs run, leap, and drag us toward Brant Hills Park. Good exercise for them, I figure, so I don't pull back too much. After all, they'll be alone till either Mr. or Mrs. Bennett returns later this afternoon when we'll be at the art gallery.

Pong jumps and twists for joy on the open field. Ping yips and nips at his heels. Faster and faster we're dragged toward the fence, where we see Mrs. Ron sitting in a lawn chair with a large moose mug in her hand.

"Hi, Mrs. Ron," I call, happy to see her without a cigar in her mouth.

"How are ya, kids?" When she sets her mug back on the patio table, I notice two things. The handle is a small set of antlers. More importantly, her coaster is a huge painted fish. Pretty sure Reuven painted the crazy Italian flag soccer ball over its middle. The fish belongs to our Stream of Dreams project.

"Great mug," I say, stalling my real question.

"Cute coaster," Renée adds, jumping right in. "Where did you get it?"

"Oh, well, our nice paper boy gave me a whole set. Said they were extras he didn't need anymore."

"The boy who delivers the *Post*?" I ask to double-check.

"Yeah, he had the fish in his wagon. What's his name again? Something to do with deli meat sandwiches …"

"Reuven?" Renée says.

"Yup, yup, yup. That's it. Ronnie's favourite. Smoked meat, Swiss cheese, Russian dressing." She laughs — *huhr, huhr, huhr!* — her broken car-engine laugh. Only the engine can't stop trying to turn over and her face turns red.

I want to scramble over the fence to help her. Only to do what? And how?

"Take a drink of tea, Mrs. Ron!" Renée hollers.

She does, and the engine sputters out. "Not tea," she rasps. "Something much better for the old ticker." She thumps her chest.

"You okay, now?" I ask.

"Yup, yup, yup."

"Okay. Well, see you at the gallery later."

"Looking forward to it. Saving my appetite for the cheese."

We wave goodbye as we chase after Ping and Pong, who gallop down the hill.

"Oh my gosh," Renée says. "Who would have suspected Reuven! Why would he steal our Stream of Dreams fish?"

"Who knows. But if he did steal the fish, maybe he also dressed up in black and helped with the garden-gnome heist," I tell her.

"Yet he was so angry with me over his dented wagon!"

"Good acting, eh?"

As we run down the hill, Ping stops at a spruce tree and starts to scold something in the branches. *Rouf, rouf, rouf.* I'm thinking it's a squirrel till I get closer and see it's another one of Red's bags of poop. I want to take it down, but I don't want to give Star more blackmail material. I stop, reach, stop, and then reach again.

"Oh, for crying out loud!" Renée leaps up and grabs it. "We are responsible pet caregivers." She runs with Ping to the garbage can in front of the library and slam-dunks it.

Then she whips out her phone. "Now for the last part of my plan. Hand me Constable Wilson's business card please."

I reach into my first aid pocket and pull it out. "What are you going to do?"

"I'm going to invite the police to the art gallery. Otherwise, what is the point of announcing the criminal?"

That is definitely mistake number three of the day, Renée loudly telling the world she is inviting the police to the gallery contest opening. Too late I see Star behind her.

DAY THREE, MISTAKE FOUR

Star wrinkles a nose that seems perfectly healed and now sports a gold ring. She's all dressed up, maybe for the gallery show, in a black miniskirt with white skull leggings and a white top. "You have no idea what kind of trouble you just caused." She shakes her fist in Renée's face.

Ping snaps and barks hysterically.

"I don't care. You're not going to get away with letting Attila take the rap for all this."

"Nothing is going to happen to Attila, you idiot. We aren't going to let it."

Ping sproings straight up in the air, snout open.

"Oh, no, you don't!" Star steps back, covering her face with her hands.

"Down, Ping!" I say and reach over to grab him.

Ping snarls low at her.

Star uncovers her face and snaps a photo with her phone. "You really should try to control your clients," she tells me, a deeply troubling smile lifting the corners of her mouth. "See you around, sucker," she says, waving as she walks back to the library. We watch her go in.

"Now what is she going to do?" I grumble.

"Don't worry. We're taking the dogs home. If she calls Animal Control, we can delay them taking Ping till we can prove she's a criminal."

"Delay taking him?" I squeak.

"Calm down. I meant totally convince them not to — who'll believe her after she's arrested?"

"Oh, okay." The dogs lead us up the hill again so that we pass by Mrs. Irwin's house and see her getting into her car. She's looking really elegant, smiling at her five Yorkies lying across the couch in front of the window. Is she whistling? I can't believe she's so happy.

Her hair is piled on her head and she's wearing a long, black dress and a trailing flowered scarf. Very dressed up for an event she believes is so unpopular.

"Guess she's off to judge the paintings," Renée says as we keep walking.

"Pretty cheerful, eh?"

Pong turns and looks wistfully toward the picture window full of Yorkies. Ping gives a hopeful bark at the dogs, who look sleepy. The Yorkies stay silent. Has Mrs. Irwin drugged them?

"Must think she's winning her bet with Mr. Kowalski."

I nod and pull Pong along. "Don't know how the two are connected, but I'm sure Bruno and Tyson's painted fish came from her recycling box."

"Wood isn't even recyclable. She's a criminal for that, for sure."

I think back to the morning we passed her house with the dogs. "Well, they might have been piled right next to it."

"Can't believe she has such a low opinion of art. Doesn't think it needs insurance." Renée shakes her head.

We reach the Bennetts' house and I chat up the team as we bring them in. "Don't you worry. Mom and Dad will be home today. You'll have company all day and night!" Ping leaps up and *roufs* as though he understands. I slip both of them a liver bite because we won't see them for a couple of days.

With their food dishes filled and bellies rubbed, they sprawl out in their dog beds and Renée and I can escape.

Just as we hit the sidewalk, Red rides by on his bike.

"Hey, you!" I call. "Stop a minute!"

"What do you want? I'm in kind of a hurry. Have to get dressed for the art show."

"You're going?" I ask.

"Yeah, my dad works at the art gallery."

"Oh, that's perfect," Renée interrupts. "Do you know that girl Star, the one who always wears the crazy tights?"

"Does she have a diamond stud in her nose?"

"Maybe a nose ring now. But yes. That's her."

"Sure. She comes to the gallery sometimes."

"Well, she reported Stephen to Animal Control for putting bags of dog doo in the trees."

"You do that, too?" he asks me. "Someone's been taking mine before I can pick them up again on the bike."

"No, Prince Clueless," Renée says. "Stephen took 'em down. Only Star snapped a photo when he was getting your poop bags. And lied to get him in trouble."

"Oh, sorry." His cheeks turn a shade lighter than his hair. "What do you want me to do?"

"Stop putting your bags in the trees, for one," I say.

"Confess," Renée adds. "Show Star up as a liar. She intends to charge Ping for biting her nose."

"Oh, no!"

"We know she stole a lawn sculpture and we're going to turn her in at the art show."

"If we do, she'll report Ping …" I start.

Renée finishes, "You telling the truth may help keep Ping alive."

"Will they fine me?" Red asks.

"No, they just warned us. But we denied the claim."

"And you only have to confess if she reports him."

"Okay, okay, I can do that. That dog is so friendly. If he bit her, she must have deserved it."

We high-five Red and he takes off. We continue on home and arrive in time to see Dad complete the last stitches on his second Yorkie sweater, the red one. "This will look great on Rose," he says as he holds it in the air for us to see.

"Good work, Mr. Noble!" Renée says. As we start knitting on our own projects, she's able to switch to a green stripe on her scarf; I'm still on the pale blue. But my rows grow more even now and I'm working faster. I hold up my four baby fingers of scarf. Doesn't look half bad, might be a Christmas present for Mom.

"You guys hungry? I'm going to fry up some bologna," Dad says when I finally reach the red stripe stage. It's his Saturday special, and even though I polished off a couple of Belgian waffles just a few hours ago, my mouth waters.

We move into the kitchen to keep him company as he cooks.

"You make the best food, Mr. Noble." Renée beams. "Fried bologna is my favourite. Can I have ketchup and peanut butter on mine?"

"What?" I gasp.

"Peanut butter on one side, ketchup on the other, bologna in the middle." She turns to Dad now. "Can I have one side of my sandwich toasted?"

"One side?" he repeats as he feeds the toaster.

"Picky, picky," I say.

"I like one side soft and one side crisp," she explains.

Dad brings a jar of peanut butter to the table and Renée carefully spreads it on a slice of bread. The toast pops and she douses her toasted slice with ketchup. Dad layers some fried bologna on top.

"Mmm," Renée says as she bites in. Then she waves her sandwich around. "Anyone want to try?"

Dad and I both take a nibble of hers and then add peanut butter and ketchup to our own sandwiches. Delicious.

"You know, Mrs. Irwin told me about one of the entries when I returned the Yorkies the other day," Dad offers as he munches. "She says someone painted an ostrich egg for the contest."

"Really?" I say.

"Yes. It's the size of a watermelon and it has a pattern of leaping fish on it in a kind of rainbow."

Renée slams her glass of milk down. "Mrs. Filipowicz!"

"Yes, yes. That's the name my client mentioned. She loves the diversity of the medium, which represents a strong segment of immigration to Burlington."

"You think her egg will win?" I ask Dad.

"Oh, I have no way of knowing. But Mrs. Irwin seemed pretty excited about it."

"Hmm. I wonder who the other judges are?"

"Another former member of the arts faculty at Mohawk. Someone from the art gallery. Also the mayor of Burlington. And the city councillor from the ward."

"Hmm. I wish there were some way to get my father to come," Renée says.

Here's where Dad makes his big mistake of the day. Number four of the day and one I make all the time — getting sucked in by oh-poor-me Renée. "Why don't I just give your parents a call? The least I could do is offer to drive your mother if she's going alone. Save on gas."

DAY THREE, MISTAKE FIVE

We hear Dad gently try to persuade Mr. Kobai to come to the art show over the phone. His conversation starts off soft but grows louder and shorter, something like this: "Yes, but … teenagers are … You're right … Yes, but … No, but …" Finally, he shouts in one whole sentence. "But he's so talented!" Then there's a lot of "Mmmhmm, hmmhmm," and then "Certainly!" and Dad hangs up.

Dad shoves another piece of fried bologna in his mouth — a sign that he's not happy — shrugs, and mumbles a meat-filled sorry to Renée.

Dad and I both head upstairs to change, leaving Renée to knit by herself. I don't know what to wear to one of these things but figure I'll go fancy seeing as my sidekick sparkles.

I own one white shirt, one dark jacket, one pair of dress pants, and dress shoes that pinch now 'cause my feet have grown since Grandpa's funeral. All of these I put on, then I call to Dad, "Can I borrow a tie?"

"Sure. Come pick."

I flip through a carousel of airplane, maple leaf, tiny checks, red hearts, and purple spot patterns to find one leaping green fish on blue silk. Looks kind of like the one I painted. I take it and Dad shows me in front of the bathroom mirror how to make a Windsor knot.

Dad looks pretty spiffy, too. He's even messed up his hair with some gel. He helps make my hair stick up, too. "Maybe we can take Mom out for dinner if she comes home on time," he says as we leave the bathroom.

When we reach the bottom of the stairs, Renée whistles.

Dad grins and bows. I roll my eyes.

We head for the Grape-mobile, what Dad calls our purple subcompact. When I open the back door, Dad calls out, "Wait a minute." He points to the seat. "Dog hair!" he says.

Of course. This is our official dog-walking car, after all, complete with the Noble Dog Walking paw print logo across the front doors.

Dad goes back in the house and comes out with a blanket, which he throws over the back seat. We sit on top of it.

Then Dad swings the Grape around to pick up Mrs. Kobai, the final clue that he could not persuade

Renée's dad to come and cheer on his son's art entry. Trying has only made things worse, I think. Renée slumps down in her seat as her mom enters.

Mrs. Kobai seems quiet and sad as she shuffles into her seat. "Thank you for the lift," she says, sniffing a bit. "Thank you, also, for having Renée for the sleepovers." You can just hear a hint of her Hungarian accent when she says the word *also*. She's a pretty lady with brown hair and eyes, but she dresses in dark colours, with none of Renée's flash or sparkle.

"No worries. She's been helping Stephen walk two of my clients so much that — I hope you don't mind, but I ordered her her own uniform."

Gah, I think.

But Renée lifts up in her seat and smiles again.

"It's good," Mrs. Kobai answers. She sniffs and changes the subject. "My husband wanted always to be an architect, you know. Instead, he studied engineering. Because of his father."

Dad nods as he drives, keeping his eyes on the road.

"Architecture is art. Our Attila should study architecture instead. It gives him such a big canvas." She opens her hands wide.

So does graffiti, I think. A high school wall sure provides a big space.

"I walk dogs," Dad tells her. "Lucky my father is dead; he wouldn't have liked that. Used to do air traffic control but the stress was getting to me."

"So many airplanes in the sky at once. Would be stressful," Mrs. Kobai agrees and then smiles. "I don't mind if Attila paints." She sighs and we ride the last few minutes to the art gallery in silence.

The Art Gallery of Burlington is an oddly shaped building right across the street from Lake Ontario. Some wings are triangular, some rectangular with floor-to-ceiling windows and grey stone. A strange orange girder structure stands outside on the western corner. *Rebecca*, it's called, after the sculptor's daughter. I learned that on one of my many class trips here when we came to make clay pots.

Today, we arrive fifteen minutes early and the parking lot already seems pretty full.

"Mrs. Irwin can't say no one is interested in art," Renée says. "Look at this."

Dad drives up and down the rows till we find a small spot near the dumpster.

Other cars seem to be cruising the streets for parking. We step out of the car and walk in through the back entrance.

Immediately inside, we face a tall display case full of green-and-blue angel sculptures, but when we walk away, I notice small, grey stone statues on top of the case.

"Wow, those are cool!" I point out the chubby boys riding tricycles to Renée.

"Yeah! Oh, check this out." She stops and reaches her hands up toward a gigantic white-and-red spider hanging above the door.

Signs for the contest direct us to the community room in the front, which means we pretty much have to tour the entire building. Yay! Along the halls, we see more sculptures, dancing cows, teapots with aliens. In the centre of the gallery, there's a garden courtyard of oversized ferns and rose-coloured blooms and sculptures. Across from it is my favourite piece: a shelf full of melting ceramic vegetables.

Lots of the art makes me smile and some of it startles me, but nothing hits me quite as hard as the first thing we see when we step into the official art contest gallery. I can't say a word, I can't even breathe.

A large screen shows Attila's tank bursting through his high school's wall.

Mrs. Kobai gasps.

The screen image pixelates and changes. Now it's a railcar with a hand grenade exploding out of the side.

Dad sucks in his breath sharply.

Renée covers her mouth with her hands. Her eyes fill. The railcar transforms into the underside of an overpass where a machine gun stretches along the cement.

Finally, the screen image changes into a large handgun painted on a water tower. "Oh, no!" Renée moans.

Is she thinking the same thing as I am? This must be Mr. Rupert's stolen handgun. Attila stole it and used it as his model.

If mistake three of the day was announcing that we were inviting the police when Star could hear us, mistake five becomes that we invited them at all. Attila's entire art collection has been illegally spray-painted on public property. Even if that gun in the painting isn't the one stolen from Mr. Rupert's house, Attila can be charged with public vandalism … again.

DAY THREE, MISTAKE SIX

Frozen, we stand watching Attila's slide show run once, twice, three times. Like being shot in the stomach with art over and over. *Weapons of Destruction*, he calls it. "War is a crime against the environment," his artist statement says. "All of these installations are located in Burlington."

"That's quite something," Dad murmurs.

"Better my husband did not come," Mrs. Kobai says.

Renée can't even talk, which is really weird for her. I have to snap her out of it, somehow. "Come on!" I tug her by the sleeve. "Let's go check out some other art."

"Yes, go ahead, kids." Dad and Mrs. Kobai wander in another direction.

Renée's feet move even though her mouth doesn't answer. We push into a crowd of elegantly dressed people, most holding wine glasses and paper plates full of fruit or crackers.

"Well, hello there!" Mrs. Ron calls. She's dressed up today. Her floor-length muumuu is sea green with brightly coloured tropical fish all over it. She waves a piece of Swiss cheese at us and swings her plate in the direction of a huge brick inukshuk. Mr. Mason's, of course. "Isn't it inspiring?"

"Very," I agree. "It's so straight ... and red." The title is *Let History Guide Us*. I read the rest of the artist's statement about reclaiming the brick from a hundred-year-old farmhouse up in northern Burlington. Included at the end is a photo of the building.

"Wow," Renée says as she stares at the inukshuk. "That must have been so heavy to carry in."

Mrs. Ron nods and smiles as if calling it heavy was a compliment. "The boys are strong. Now, don't forget to vote for your favourite piece of art!"

"Sure, we will. Where are the ballots?" I ask.

"Over in that corner." She waves her cheese again.

"We'll just look at the others before we vote," I tell her.

"This one's the best." She winks at us. "Trust me." She pops the rest of the cheese into her mouth and nods.

On one wall, there's a series of photos of sunrises over the pier. *Beginnings in Burlington*, the artist calls it.

"Pretty," I say out loud.

A woman dressed all in black and wearing spikey tall boots turns around. "Why, thank you, Stephen!"

"You're welcome, Mrs. Watier," I answer our principal. She's such a hurry-up-take-charge kind of person, who knew she could stand still long enough to take pictures?

We continue along that wall to see a table covered with rocks and tiny green plants. *Bonsai on the Escarpment* the title reads.

"Wow. Itsy-bitsy trees," Renée says as she leans her head in.

"Careful, not too close, please," Mr. Jirad says. "Bonsai is to encourage contemplation. Not touching!"

"That's such an interesting take of a local landscape," Mrs. Irwin says from behind us.

"Oh, thank you, thank you, Madam." He nods his head in a mini bow. "I grafted from small trees actually growing on the site."

"Is that even legal?" Renée asks me. "Isn't that a conservation area?"

I elbow her. "He is conserving. Just look."

"Cheese, anyone?"

We turn from the bonsai display to see Reuven holding out a plate of Gouda and Swiss.

"You stole the fish from our Stream of Dreams project, didn't you?" Renée hisses at him.

Reuven shakes his head.

"We saw the ones you gave Mrs. Ron. She was using them as coasters."

Reuven pulls us aside and lowers his voice. "I found the fish in the wagon. I thought you stole them."

"Why would we steal the fish and then just leave them?" I ask.

"I don't know. All of them weren't there."

Renée rolls her eyes at him. "Why didn't you report us, then?"

"I wasn't sure … and I didn't want to cause trouble." He hesitates for a suspicious half-second, but then covers it up with anger. "Why would you just take my wagon and break it?"

Mr. Jirad hears his son. And who doesn't? Reuven accuses us loudly enough. His dad shakes a finger at him. "Don't worry so much about that piece of junk."

"Yeah, but they took it without even asking!" Reuven gripes.

"They did not break it!" Mr. Jirad scolds. "And we can find you another one next trash day."

One of Renée's eyebrows twitches. Did she hear the same thing as I did? How does Mr. Jirad know that we didn't make the dent in the middle of Reuvan's wagon? And why was Reuven unsure about turning the wooden fish evidence in to the police? Was he protecting someone else?

At that moment, Mrs. Whittingham's little boy, August, reaches out to touch one of the tiny shrubs and Mr. Jirad calls out to him, "No, no, no!"

We take that moment to drift away. "Great trees, anyway," Renée calls back to Mr. Jirad.

I hold up two thumbs in agreement. Then I whisper to her, "He ignores conservation law. And he knows we didn't wreck Reuven's wagon."

"Very suspicious," she agrees.

As we move down the wall, we bump into Star.

"If it isn't baby sister," she says when she sees Renée. "You saw Attila's art, I presume?"

"Yes," Renée answers miserably.

"Oh, come on. It's easily the best work in the room. Will you look at this wall hanging?"

We all face a fabric picture of an old church I recognize from up on Highway 5.

"*God Lives Here in Burlington*," Star reads the title out loud and shakes her head. "Not sure she does."

"I like it," I say, wanting to disagree with her.

Renée stays quiet.

"You can't expect a talent like Attila to colour within the lines, can you?" Star asks.

Renée shrugs and frowns.

"And the police didn't come, so all is good." She smiles and sips from her wineglass.

"The police didn't come," Renée repeats. "My father didn't, either." She brightens.

"So go have some munchies and just enjoy!" Star swings her wineglass around.

A small mistake. Could be number six of the day. At that moment, Mrs. Whittingham's son, August, runs into us full speed. Renée gets shoved into me, I get pushed into Star, and her wineglass flies from her hand.

It's amazing just how far sparkling red cranberry juice can travel! The red liquid splashes all over us, of course, but much of it sprays over the wall hanging.

The little church looks like it's bleeding.

Star and Renée and I rush to the snack area for napkins. That's when we realize easily our biggest error of the day, the real sixth mistake: thinking Attila's graffiti display would not be noticed by the law.

Because at that moment, Constables Wilson and Jurgensen stroll in and stop. Both look up to the large screen. And in that exact moment, the slide of the gun on the water tower appears.

DAY THREE, MISTAKE SEVEN

Renée whimpers as she dabs away cranberry juice from her face and arms.

"It'll be okay, really it will." I try to make her believe the words even as we both see Constable Jurgensen scowl and shake his head.

"Do you think they'll wait till the show's over to take my brother away?"

"Oh, for sure," I lie. "Where is Attila, anyway? Maybe they won't even see him."

"I don't know. There's a big crowd over there." She points her chin at the other wall.

"Yeah, there he is, all right. I see his mohawk sticking up over the crowd." I shrug. "Maybe he'll win the competition and the judge will go easy."

Renée groans. "In England, a judge sentenced Kristian Holmes to three and a half years."

"Who is Kristian Holmes?" I ask.

"Another graffiti artist — has two little kids."

"Ohhhh." I wipe at the cranberry juice on my own shirt. Doesn't look like the stain is coming out.

Then I notice Mr. Kowalski moving through the crowd. He stops at the wall hanging. In his hand he holds a can of club soda. I hear a pop as he removes the tab, then gasps all around as he pitches soda over the bleeding church.

At his side, a muscular lady with lots of curls all over her head covers her face with her hands.

Renée and I walk closer to watch.

Mr. Kowalski stands back a moment, as if waiting, and then steps forward and dabs at the wall hanging with paper towel.

Slowly, the red stain disappears. Within a couple of minutes, the wall hanging looks back to its old self.

The lady throws her arms around Mr. Kowalski and hugs him.

"Soda works," I tell Renée. "I'm going to try some on my shirt." I wait till the woman releases Mr. Kowalski. She looks familiar.

"Mr. Kowalski, may I try some of that club soda on this stain?" I touch the wet patch on the front of my shirt.

The woman turns toward me.

Mr. Kowalski hands me the can. "Kids, this is Janet Lacey. The artist who created this wonderful wall hanging."

The Animal Control officer!

"Hi," I say as Renée takes the soda from me. She pitches some onto the red stain on my front.

"Wait till it bubbles," Mr. Kowalski advises, then hands her some paper towel. "Now try to soak it up. Don't rub!" he cautions.

Renée carefully dabs. The red becomes pink then, amazingly, my shirt turns white again.

"Were they the ones who spilled their drink on my art?" Ms. Lacey asks.

"No, it was her!" Renée points with the pop can toward Star, who weaves and dodges smoothly through the crowd like a dancer. Or, like someone who wants to hide.

"The one with the hoop through her nose?" Ms. Lacey asks.

Renée nods hard and grins.

"Well, I guess I need to talk to her."

"It was an accident," Mr. Kowalski calls to her back. She storms off without hearing.

"What are you doing?" I ask Renée as we watch Ms. Lacey grab Star's shoulder.

"What do you think?" She grins at me and her eyebrows stretch up to smile, too. "Whose side will Animal Control be on if Ms. Lacey thinks Star trashed her wall hanging?"

Star's eyes drift our way and Renée waves.

"She'll just explain about August bumping into her and everything will be all right."

Ms. Lacey shakes a finger in Star's face.

"Maybe not," Renée says.

Star's eyes narrow as she fixes her stare on me. I shrug my shoulders.

For sure, everything Renée does makes Star dislike me more. Will that end badly for Ping?

"Ignore her, Stephen. Come on, let's look over

there." Renée points to a pedestal sitting in the centre of the room. We stroll over and wait for some people to move away. Finally, they leave and we can move in to see.

"The ostrich egg!" Renée exclaims.

The large egg shimmers from inside a glass case, specks of glitter on the shell catching the light. The rainbow of fish painted across it looks exactly like the ones from our Stream of Dreams — well, minus the two larger ones Bruno and Tyson painted.

"Doesn't that prove she stole the fish?" I whisper to Renée. "At least Attila's off the hook for that."

"I don't know," Renée grumbles. "Are the police anywhere?"

We both look around. "Still staring at Attila's slides," I tell her. Someone bumps into me as I turn back. "Oh, Mrs. Filipowicz, hi!"

Our crossing guard looks tiny without her bulky coat on. Her crow-wing black hair has been styled into corkscrews and she looks way softer. I wouldn't recognize her if she hadn't told us about her egg sculpture before.

"Hello. You like it?" she asks us. She smiles at the egg like a mother ostrich.

"You took the fish and told the police we did," Renée snaps, charming as always.

"Oh, no!" She turns. "I took the peecture on my phone." She pantomimes holding up a cellphone and pressing down. "Then I look at it to paint my *pisanka: School Children of Burlington*." She waves an imaginary paintbrush in the air.

"But the painting is missing two fish," I say. "Exactly the ones the dogs took from the recycling bin across from the school."

"You used your all-purpose screwdriver," Renée suggests.

"Ees very handy." She holds up her hands. "Okay. Okay! You *heve* me over the barrel on those. The bass and the swordfeesh, yes, I took. So big and such sloppy painting! Ruin everything for me!"

"But you didn't steal the rest?" I ask.

"No. I don't steal! Just tidied a beet." She smiles at her egg again. "Do you like my *pisanka*?"

"Very much," I say.

"Lovely," Renée growls.

"You can vote for eet. Ballots are over there." She points to the corner.

"Thanks. Need to look at all the exhibits first, only fair," I say as I steer Renée away. I glance back to the door and see Constables Wilson and Jurgensen still watching Attila's slides. "You stay here," I tell Renée. "I'm going to talk to the police."

"What? No. I'm coming. Attila's my brother!"

"Don't take this the wrong way. But I don't think you'll help him. You have a way of irritating them."

"I irritate them? You're the one who didn't tell them about the bass and swordfish until they made you empty your pockets."

As always, she has a point. Neither of us made a good impression on the two constables. "Come on, then. Could you maybe just let me do the talking?" I don't wait for an answer as we both make our way back to the entrance of the room. I lower my voice as we get closer to them. "Can you also not bring up exploding Reuven's backpack?"

"I won't say a word."

"Hi, Constables. Are you planning to take Attila away?" I ask.

Renée elbows me hard.

"Why would we do that?" Constable Jurgensen asks. "He's out on bail right now. Does he look like a flight risk?"

"No, no! He's not going to make a break for it. I just thought because he painted that gun on the water tower." I point to the slide as it comes up again.

"No one's complained," Constable Wilson says and we both stare at the gun. "Pretty realistic, isn't it?"

"You'd swear it was going to fire on us, wouldn't you?" Constable Jurgensen says.

Constable Wilson nods. "But just because Attila has a photo on a slide doesn't mean he personally vandalized a water tower."

"I don't even know where that tower is," Constable Jurgensen says. "Do you?" he asks his partner.

"Nope. Probably not in our jurisdiction." She smiles.

I guess neither read the artist's statement.

"Yes, but he painted a gun, which could mean he used Mr. Rupert's as a model," I say, wondering why they're both so nice all of a sudden.

Renée kicks me this time. "He could have used a picture!" I knew she couldn't last. "Maybe Attila took his image from the internet."

"Maybe," Constable Jurgensen says. "'Cause the one on the tower is a semi-automatic. The one we found in the school library is a revolver. An older model."

"An antique really. I would have thought he'd paint the one he stole," Constable Wilson says.

"Be a convenient model, for sure," Constable Jurgensen agrees.

"Makes me wonder if he's innocent," Constable Wilson says.

Renée just can't help herself. "Attila didn't steal Mr. Rupert's mailbox, either." Her voice grows louder as she defends him, mistake number seven of the day. No one ever believes you when you shout. "Attila was trying to put the mailbox back." Renée's words cut through all the chatter in the gallery. "It's his girlfriend who took it. She's somewhere in this room." Around us, conversations seem to stop as Renée's tone turns shrill. Everyone stops to look at us as she continues. "You should arrest …"

DAY THREE, MISTAKE EIGHT

She's planning to announce the criminal later, anyway. I don't know why I tense up. That's what she told some people to convince them to come to the show today. Although most of them didn't need convincing. Most of the suspects seem to be artists who were planning to attend, anyway.

"Go on, whom should we arrest?" Constable Jurgensen asks.

"What she means to say" — I lower my voice and wait for people go back to their own conversations — "is that there are so many other people who could be involved in the art heists."

"Art heists?" Constable Jurgensen says.

"Yes," I whisper. "Our crossing guard just admitted to removing the swordfish and bass from our Stream of Dreams."

"That leaves a couple hundred others," Constable Jurgensen says.

"We have reason to believe Mr. Jirad might know something about them. Someone left a bunch of our fish in his son's wagon."

"Mrs. Ron over there uses them as coasters," Renée adds.

Constable Jurgensen scratches his head now.

Constable Wilson just smiles.

"You have to wonder about anyone's motive," I say. "Why does someone want a mailbox that looks like Mr. Rupert's house?"

"Or a bunch of painted wooden fish?" Renée pipes in.

"Or a sculpture of Grumpy? Although I really like it myself."

Constable Jurgensen gives me the stink eye.

"But I would never steal it," I quickly add. "C'mon, they're our neighbours. They might notice if their lawn ornament ended up in our yard."

"It's the gun left behind in the school we're most concerned with," says Constable Wilson.

Speaking of Grumpy … suddenly, from out of the crowd in the other corner, a loud voice booms, "Oh my God!"

"You'll excuse us," Constable Wilson says, and she and Constable Jurgensen turn toward that voice.

"Follow them." Renée grabs me by the hand before I can agree, and we become their tails as they bustle through the museum guests.

A bunch of people stand gaping in front of a large exhibit.

"Maybe you should have your cellphone ready," I tell Renée. After all, she took a picture when Reuven's backpack exploded in the sandbox.

We move past the centre of the room to where I see most of our neighbours crowded around the exhibit: Mr. Jirad, Mrs. Watier, Mr. Kowalski, Mrs. Whittingham and August, my father, Renée's mom, even the Lebels with their white-haired children, and we didn't even invite them. Mrs. Klein stands next to Mr. Rupert, one hand on his back, rubbing it.

"The installation is really quite remarkable. *Stolen Art* it's called," Mrs. Irwin explains. "But it's … not classical art … more everyday."

Finally, we break through and see the display.

Our fish! Grumpy! Mrs. Whittingham's dead baby doll and Halloween raven!

"That's my wife's art!" Mr. Rupert's voice moans.

He's right. His mailbox sits on one side of the installation. Will he kill someone now? We push closer and I see his mouth hanging open. Mrs. Klein drapes her arm over his shoulder.

"She finished this one at the hospice." Mr. Rupert sounds like a wounded animal, a dog, maybe. "It was her best work." He pulls out a handkerchief from his pocket and blows his nose loudly like a trumpet.

"The detail is incredible," Mrs. Klein says. "It looks exactly like your house."

"That's our Halloween baby doll," a kid whines from next to us. It's August, twirling a strand of his hair between his thumb and forefinger.

Mrs. Whittingham nods. "Yes, they took our display without asking. Kind of rude." She digs her fists into her hips.

"I like my swing empty," August says. "So I can use it."

Mrs. Whittingham shrugs, steps back, and crosses her arms over her chest. "Really interesting, I have to say."

Our Stream of Dreams fish, except for the swordfish, bass, and Mrs. Ron's coasters, "swim" from wires that hold them to the ceiling in the same rainbow shape as they were in on the school fence. Under one side of the arc, the Halloween stuff and the Grumpy sculpture stand, grim and grey. On the other, that one beautiful mailbox-house sits. But it brightens up the whole display, giving it a sense of love and home.

"I wish I could have known Mrs. Rupert," Renée says out loud.

Mr. Rupert honks his nose again.

I read the artist's statement out loud. "'A world with and without art,' signed 'the Burlington Group of Four.'" Underneath is a silhouette of four people shaded out in black.

"I wonder who they are," Mrs. Klein says.

"A real mystery," Red, our grade eight friend says.

"Not to me," Renée brags loudly.

This is mistake eight, similar to mistake seven when she was too loud about defending Attila. But in this case, she may be taunting our criminal, forcing his or her hand, which is not quite the same. Everyone turns to look at her.

Near the mailbox side of the fish, Star stands right next to Ms. Lacey, the Animal Control officer. She doesn't look angry with her anymore. They actually look pretty chummy.

"Once the speeches are done," Renée continues, "I will announce their names. They stole all the pieces to their art installation, after all."

Star squints at me and frowns, then takes out her cellphone, leans over to Ms. Lacey, and says something in her ear. Oh, come on! Is she really showing her the photo of her nose wound, the one poor Ping accidentally caused?

Ping may be facing big trouble because of Renée's announcement.

DAY THREE, MISTAKE NINE

I pull Renée as far away from Star as possible, for her own safety, as well as my own. "C'mon, let's go get a ballot."

"Maybe some grapes and cheese, too."

"Sure." I glance around as we walk, waving at Dad's Rottweiler client. "I don't see your brother anywhere. Do you?"

"No, but your dad just walked over to the punch bowl."

We join him. Dad sips at some red liquid from a glass cup.

"Did you vote already?" Renée asks.

"Yes. There was no doubt in my mind about the best piece of art here." Dad makes a fist against his chest. "You feel it right inside you."

Renée smiles as she rips off a couple of pieces of paper.

"Do you need a pen?" Dad asks and hands me one.

Renée and I both write down *Weapons of Destruction*. It's not even because Attila is her brother. Dad's right. There's no way you can look at the slides and not feel something.

"Where's my mother?" Renée asks.

Dad nods in the direction of our two police officers, who look almost as though they are guarding the *Stolen Art* exhibit. Mrs. Kobai shuffles through the crowd behind them.

I spread some brie on a cracker. "Here." I give it to Renée. "High-fat dairy can be soothing."

She takes it and nibbles. "It is very good."

I spread a cracker for myself and then put it down immediately when Renée starts choking.

"Can you breathe?" She's doubled over, hacking into her hand.

I reach both arms around her, ready to perform the Heimlich.

"Stop … yes," she rasps. "My father just walked in."

I release her and look toward the door. A tall man in a dark suit stands, arms crossed, watching the slides of *Weapons of Destruction*. His frown reminds me of Attila's. He's tough looking, too, except his head, which is completely shaved, shaped like a bullet, and shining in the light.

"Your attention, everybody." Mrs. Irwin taps at a microphone near the back of the room. "Please make sure you have your ballots in for the People's Choice Award. We're going to be counting those votes in a moment."

Renée and I fold our slips of paper and move toward the ballot box. We wait as others slide their votes in.

"I'm voting for *Stolen Art*," Mr. Rupert says loudly. "My wife's mailbox is the most beautiful piece in the room."

"Mmm." Mrs. Klein stares up at the hand grenade on the railcar slide, her mouth moving in a kind of I-can't-decide Watusi. She holds a ballot in her hand. It still appears blank. "So much talent in Burlington," she says. "I love the graffiti slides. Those weapons painted so big and bold … well, they just make me shiver."

Mr. Rupert grumbles something in her ear.

"She likes weapons?" I whisper to Renée.

"She likes a guy who runs around in a camouflage uniform, too," she whispers back.

Mrs. Klein's companion turkey, or maybe companion soldier, is Mr. Rupert. She was afraid at night in the school after that car crashed into the building a couple of weeks ago. Mr. Rupert makes her feel safe; who can blame her?

He sure doesn't make me feel safe, though. Especially, I don't want him to meet up with the Burlington Group of Four, although at least the police have his gun. Or at least I think they've kept it as evidence.

A red-haired man in a jacket with a name tag comes and picks up the ballot box.

"Just one more second, young man!" Mrs. Klein calls. She bends over the table and scribbles something on her ballot.

The man doesn't look all that young. Judging by the colour of hair, I think he's Red's dad. Red told us he worked here.

Finally, Mrs. Klein folds it and pops it into the slot on the top of the box. "Thank you, dearie, you can take it now."

He smiles and offers the box around. "Anybody else?" He waits for a moment but there are no more voters. "All right, then." He walks away.

"Everyone, everyone," Mrs. Irwin calls. "Please fill up your glasses and plates and then draw around. The presentations are about to begin."

I grab a stack of whole-grain crackers and slice off a mound of goat cheese. Renée's mouth looks like a squeezed lemon, so I have a feeling she needs more dairy de-stressing.

People gather closer to the front of the room

"Ladies and gentlemen, may I present Mayor Silverring."

Everyone applauds enthusiastically. I can't, though, not with the plate in my hand. Dad and Mrs. Kobai stand near Mr. Jirad's bonsai escarpment art and we join them. Mr. Kobai stays at the back.

"You know a city not by its factories or stores. Or even by its houses or condo high-rises or roads and sidewalks." He goes on for a while about all the things you don't know a city by, and I duck behind Dad to spread some cheese on crackers. I pass one to Renée and munch on one myself.

Finally, he finishes with, "You know a city by its art."

"And the people who create that art …"

People clap again.

"Today, our community has come together to celebrate art that speaks directly to it, art that we have made ourselves, about ourselves."

This time I hold the plate in my teeth and clap along with the crowd.

"I now pass the microphone back to Jessica Irwin, Mohawk College's esteemed dean of art. She will present the prizes for this year's show."

The room breaks into applause again and Mrs. Irwin smiles as she takes the mayor's place.

"Thank you, thank you, thank you. I am so happy to see all of you out here. Art does not feed or clothe our bodies but it does feed and clothe our souls. I am so glad you recognize this and have come out to celebrate our own soul food."

"And soul clothes," Renée whispers to me.

"In the past, I have been discouraged by the lack of value placed on music, literature, and art, but today, today, I am proven wrong.

"I would like to call up my colleague Mr. William Kowalski."

While the others are clapping, Renée and I eat the last of the crackers. There's only a small bump of cheese left now.

Mr. Kowalski finally makes it through the crowd, and Mrs. Irwin gives him a big, long hug. Not sure whether she's secretly choking him. Then she breaks away and speaks into the mic again.

"William and I have a bet, you see — which I believe he cheated on." She wags her finger at him. "I bet him that no one would ever steal the art we had in our staff room. That no one stole art anymore. The loser would add five hundred dollars to the prize for the winner of the art contest. Behind me today is direct proof that I have lost that bet: the *Stolen Art* exhibit; although I feel he may have orchestrated the stealing of that art. Nevertheless, the fact that you are all here also backs up the heart of his bet, which is quite simply that people do indeed value art. This is a bet I am so happy to lose. So I want you all to witness Bill receiving my cheque made out to the winner of the art show this year."

There are whistles and whoops as she pulls out an envelope and hands it to him.

"Would you kindly read out the name on the cheque and the winner of this year's Burlington Art Award?"

Mr. Kowalski smiles as he tears open the envelope. His smile grows even bigger when he looks at the cheque. "The winner is Attila Kobai for *Weapons of Destruction*."

Mistake number nine of the day turns out to be when Renée throws her arms around me and hugs me — forgetting all about that bit of goat cheese left on the plate between us.

DAY THREE, MISTAKE TEN

Somehow enough white crumbly cheese squishes over both of our shirts that we look like a seagull dumped on us. Renée shrugs her shoulders. "Sorry."

I roll my eyes and shake my head. But then, I forget everything and turn to watch as Attila saunters up to accept his prize. He's dressed in a black shirt and skinny jeans with boots, a formal look for him. When he gets close enough, Mrs. Irwin reaches out and shakes his hand, then gives him the cheque, as well as a framed certificate. She gestures toward him and smiles. The audience applauds and Attila gives a quick, small head bow. His mouth remains straight as an arrow.

As Mrs. Kobai snaps a picture with her phone, Renée turns around to look at her father. Her eyebrows knit. I turn, too. Mr. Kobai's arms remain folded across his chest. His mouth stays as straight as Attila's. Neither are big smilers, I guess.

I can hear Renée sigh as we both turn back to watch the presentation of the other prizes.

Mrs. Irwin continues. "Taking second place is …" She pauses for drama and then rushes the words. "Barbara Filipowicz for *School Children of Burlington.*"

Madame X shrieks with joy.

Well, that's more like it.

We clap madly along with everyone else.

Mrs. Filipowicz marches crossing-guard style to the front and receives an envelope and certificate. She lines up beside Attila.

"Third place is … Azid Jirad for *Bonsai on the Escarpment.*"

Mr. Jirad does a little dance, runs up, and high-fives Mrs. Filipowicz. They both turn to Attila, who nods and shakes their hands.

Red's dad steps in from a backroom and whispers something into Mrs. Irwin's ear. Her eyebrows shoot up.

She leans toward the microphone. "Ladies and gentlemen, there will be a short delay as we recount the votes for the People's Choice Award. At this point, it seems we may have a tie."

"Ohhh." Immediately, everyone starts to talk in hushed tones so that it sounds like the buzz of bees on a hot summer day.

"Let's see if we can get this off now," Renée says to me, pointing to the smear of goat cheese on her shirt. We head for the family washroom together.

Inside, we tear off paper towel, wet it, and wipe at the cheese. The whiteness seems to roll off. "Wish we had some more club soda."

Side by side, we stand and stare into the mirrors at the dark spots left behind — water or cheesy oil, only time will tell.

A toilet suddenly flushes and Ms. Lacey steps out.

"About that wound on Star's nose …" I start to explain.

"It wasn't Ping's fault," Renée finishes. "Star bent down and encouraged him to kiss her."

"Who's Ping?" Ms. Lacey asks as she lifts her shirt and dabs a piece of cotton against her belly button.

I grab Renée's arm to stop her talking. "Ms. Lacey, can I ask, um … what you are doing?"

"Putting some Aspirin paste on my keloid. Caught my belly button ring on my jean snap …"

"Star showed you her nose on her phone," I start again.

"And suggested this cure for keloids," Ms. Lacey finishes. "I had some aspirin in my purse."

I see the cotton has an aspirin in it. Not quite paste yet. I put my finger to my lips to signal to Renée that she shouldn't say anything else about Ping. Clearly, Star did not report him. Yet.

"Good luck with that," I say and we leave the bathroom. Through the open gallery door, I notice Mr. Kobai has moved up closer to the front. He's standing next to Renée's mom now.

"Does my father look the least bit pleased that Attila won the art prize?" Renée asks when she notices him.

"Well, honestly, no. But neither does Attila. They look a lot alike, don't they?"

"Sort of," Renée agrees.

"Do they act alike?"

"Sometimes." Her mouth twists. "You're right. This is hopeless. They're never going to get along." She droops her head.

"I didn't say that. I just meant that maybe on the inside, they're both doing the yay-yay-happy-art-prize dance. They just don't show it on the outside." I touch her shoulder. "Come on. Let's go see who won the People's Choice."

Just before we enter the gallery again, we pass some flying cow sculptures. "Look, Renée!"

She finally smiles again. The power of art.

We make it back just in time. Hanging with Dad is a woman in a navy skirt and jacket and a red vest. She's leaning in to him a little too chummy, if you ask me.

"Mom!" I call.

She turns toward me, smiles, and opens her arms.

I rush to her, not caring who's watching, and give her a big hug.

"Your attention, everyone," Mrs. Irwin calls into the microphone. "We have counted twice. It's official now. The tally of the votes for the People's Choice Award shows a tie! We have decided to award two exhibits with our People's Choice Award, this year … *Stolen Art* by the Burlington Group of Four and … *Weapons of Destruction* by Attila Kobai."

Mrs. Irwin and Attila shake hands again as he accepts a second cheque and envelope.

Everyone claps, Mr. Kobai, too, even if he doesn't smile.

"We're about to find out who stole Mr. Rupert's mailbox and Mrs. Whittingham's Halloween decorations," I whisper to Renée. "Would the Group of Four step forward?" Mrs. Irwin calls.

No one comes to the front. "I really want to emphasize that these artists taught me the value of art in our everyday households, both through their creation but also in the reactions of those who had their art stolen from them. I look forward to meeting them." She taps her foot, looks around, sighs heavily. "Surely, someone knows who these four artists are," Mrs. Irwin says. "Who registered the work?"

"This is my chance. I'm going to reveal the thieves' identities," Renée says to me. "Ping should be fine as long as the police take them to the station right away."

Renée walks to the microphone, covers it with her hand, and talks to Mrs. Irwin.

"Mom, I'm going up there to be with Renée."

"Sure. Go for it, Stephen."

Renée adjusts the microphone so it's way lower, at her height, then taps the microphone three times: *pock, pock, pock.*

"Ladies and gentlemen, the Burlington Group of Four are Star Loughead, Mr. Jirad, Mr. Kowalski — he arranged everything — and, finally, my own brother, Attila Kobai.

"The real question is, who stole Mr. Rupert's gun? It wasn't Attila. I know that in my heart. I'm guessing it was one of you ..."

I jump in. "I know who did it!"

Renée looks drop-dead amazed. She stares at me.

The answer seems obvious to me. It's the only solution that makes sense. I step forward and adjust the microphone back up. "No one!"

"What do you mean 'no one'?" she asks.

"Mr. Rupert dropped the gun in the school. By accident. He was checking out the building because Mrs. Klein heard a noise and called him again."

"I thought I saw ninjas sneaking around the school," Mrs. Klein pipes in.

Mr. Rupert turns to her, looking confused. "You didn't tell me I dropped my revolver in the school."

"I didn't get a chance," Mrs. Klein says.

The crowd murmurs, "Ohhhh."

He turns and snarls at them, "Give me a break. It's a non-firing replica!"

"Things happened so fast," Mrs. Klein continues. "The librarian found the gun and called the police."

Our principal, Mrs. Watier, pushes her way through the crowd. "But you let us continue the lockdown."

"I'm so sorry. I thought the officers would know it was a fake. I didn't want to get in trouble for having Mr. Rupert in the school with me."

Mr. Rupert turns back to the crowd, his hands open wide. "I never intended to hurt anyone. Not even a ninja."

"The lockdown scared all of us," I tell Mrs. Klein. Her mistake, not stopping it right away, a bad one, I think. Adults make them all the time, too, not just kids. I wonder if it will cost Mrs. Klein her job and maybe even her new boyfriend.

"Mr. Rupert had my brother arrested," Renée complains.

"Maybe he didn't steal my gun but he did steal my wife's mailbox," he grumbles back.

"You never told the police it was a replica gun, either," Renée adds.

"I told the desk sergeant it was a copy of my daddy's World War Two Browning HP!" Mr. Rupert answers. "Thought that was a pretty accurate description."

"He couldn't have told the investigating officers," Mrs. Klein says.

"Maybe they held back that detail to catch the criminal," Renée suggests.

Mr. Rupert turns tomato-soup red. Looks like he wants to blast someone.

I change the subject to calm him down. "I guess you'll be wanting that mailbox back now," I say.

He shakes his head. "You know, I don't. All her life, my wife wanted to be an artist and have an exhibit at this very building." He looks around the room, nodding and smiling.

"Now she has her mailbox here," I say.

"That's right. I think she would have wanted it that way."

"So I guess you have Attila Kobai to thank for that, seeing as he took the mailbox for this exhibit."

Renée starts, "But I think —"

"Tst!" I put my finger to my lips. "Ping, remember?" I ask her softly.

But there's never any stopping Renée when she has an idea.

She pushes me aside and lowers the microphone again. "I believe my brother was returning the mailbox. That his girlfriend, his *former* girlfriend," she emphasizes, "Star Loughead, took it and he's just covering up for her."

I sidle back into position and bend down over the microphone like a giraffe going in for a drink. "Is that how it really happened, Attila?"

Attila shakes his head, takes two strides, and also hip-checks me out of the way. He adjusts the microphone higher, *ahem, ahems* for a while, and then says, "It is true. I am one of the four." He pauses as the audience settles back down. "And I would like to thank William Kowalski and my fellow artists Star Loughead and Mr. Jirad, the other three. Please join me in congratulating them with a round of applause." To a thunder of handclapping, Mr. Kowalski and Mr. Jirad shuffle back to the front. Star takes a while longer to straggle up. Attila waits and smiles. "While Mr. Kowalski instructed us to take something that really means something to us, I take full responsibility for the stealing of Mr. Rupert's mailbox. I have admired that piece of art on Mr. Rupert's door from the time he hung it up. I deeply regret that Mrs. Rupert died before achieving the fame she justly deserves. I confess, I took that mailbox because it belonged in our exhibit! It completed it. I apologize for any hurt this theft may have caused Mr. Rupert."

Mr. Rupert again honks his nose into a handkerchief. Mrs. Klein leans her head on his shoulder but he pulls away.

Even though Constables Wilson and Jurgensen said they weren't going to take Attila away, they now part the crowd to march to the front.

Renée gasps.

None of the art owners seem unhappy with the fact that their pieces are part of a larger display of art. Especially since it won the grand prize. Even Mr. Rupert seems pleased. None of them are going to press charges, I'm sure of it.

But the constables don't approach Attila or any of the other art burglars. Instead they surround Mr. Rupert.

"I am arresting you, Thomas Rupert, for carrying an imitation of a weapon for a purpose dangerous to public peace," Constable Jurgensen says.

"What danger? I only showed it her," Mr. Rupert sputters, pointing to Mrs. Klein.

"Tell it to the judge." Constable Wilson reaches for Mr. Rupert's hands and cuffs them. "You have the right to retain counsel ..."

Mrs. Klein starts to cry.

"You have the right to remain silent," Constable Jurgensen continues.

Just when I thought everything was going to end well for everyone. Mistake ten, the worst one for days, belongs to Mr. Rupert, who thought a replica gun couldn't do any harm. It sure was dangerous to our school's peace.

The constables lead Mr. Rupert outside, with Mrs. Klein following them.

the
aftermath

The room stays quiet for a moment, the celebration feels over.

Then, grinning as wide as a keyboard, Dad steps up to congratulate Attila. He wraps Mrs. Kobai in a hug and reaches a hand toward Mr. Kobai, who hesitates, his lip twitching for a second. Finally he returns the handshake.

"Would you like to join us for dinner?" Dad asks the Kobais. He's bringing some of the celebratory feeling back to the room.

"No." Mr. Kobai bites off his words. "It is time for our daughter and son to return home. We need to discuss everything that occurred." His *r*'s roll, a bit of a Hungarian burr.

I'm relieved, actually. Sorry for Renée. She has to go home with that angry man, maybe listen to him lecture her brother.

But I'm happy to not have to share Mom's attention, 'cause let's face it, Renée always demands that little extra with her sparkle and her cross-examinations. "See you tomorrow, Renée?"

It'll be Sunday and we don't have any dog-walking duties at all together. What am I thinking?

"That would be great! Maybe we can play Ping-Pong at Brant Hills," she answers brightly. "Seeing as we won't be walking them."

"I'll probably be finished reading *The Night Gardener* by tomorrow, too. I can bring it for you."

"Okay. See you."

The Kobais leave and Dad suggests we cross the street to eat at Spencer's Landing since we're so dressed up.

"Mmm. You two are salted caramel for the eyes." Mom sighs. "But I'm still in my uniform and feel grotty. Also, I would love some of your meat loaf," she says to Dad. "Do you have any ready?"

"You're in luck. I froze some leftovers."

"Perfect. And your salad?" she says to me.

"Okay," I agree. "I wouldn't mind ditching these shoes, either. They're killing me."

So we head for home, just the three of us, and I inhale Momness all the way in the car. She smells like apple and cinnamon.

"So tell us how you figured out who stole all the art in the neighbourhood?" Mom asks as Dad drives.

"The key was Reuven's wagon. It's a low-sided red metal job. His dad found it on junk day."

"Yes?" Dad says, as we pull up to a red light.

"How did the wagon help you pull all this together?" Mom asks.

"We saw some kids, Mrs. Klein's ninjas, pulling it late at night in the schoolyard. I mean the same kind of wagon with the low sides."

"Most people have those oversized plastic ones," Dad says.

"Right. And next day, Reuven complained that someone had dented his. Later, he found some of our Stream of Dreams fish in it but didn't report it."

The light changes and we pull away.

"Well, that's ridiculous," Mom says. "Why wouldn't he when he knew the police were involved?"

I shrug my shoulders. "He claimed he thought it was us. I knew his dad drove Mr. Kowalski's van. Knew that Mr. Kowalski coached Attila on his portfolio. Attila is applying to Mohawk College's art program. A lot of unexplained connections."

"All leading to Mohawk College," Mom adds.

"You're right. Star already attends Mohawk. She's the one who lost that black cap in the schoolyard. Renée figured her for one of the kids stealing the art."

"But Jirad and Kowalski aren't kids," Dad says.

"True enough. Small enough builds to be mistaken for teens, though. Let's face it, any kind of theft or vandalism always gets blamed on kids. This time, that would only be partly correct. In the dark, dressed in black, who can tell?"

"Why would Kowalski do something so irresponsible?" Mom says.

Dad stops for another red light. "Does seem wrong for a teacher to behave that way."

"He had a bet with Mrs. Irwin over the value of art. And man, he is a competitive kind of guy. Have you seen him play Ping-Pong. Or jog?"

"Did I hear her say she didn't think the public valued art anymore?" Dad asks.

"Yes, she bet Mr. Kowalski that they didn't need to insure the staff room art. That no one would steal art."

"Wow, a dean of art who doesn't believe in the value of art," Mom says.

"She even put his painting out with the trash. That's the one Dad scooped for the guest room. Wait till you see it, Mom. You'll love it."

"I know I will. The gun — how did you figure out that Mr. Rupert dropped it?" Mom asks.

"He had Attila charged for the theft of his gun the day of the lockdown. So we knew he had one. And he's always checking the school grounds for Mrs. Klein."

"Green light," Mom calls at Dad and we pull away again.

"Ever since that VW drove into the building," I continue explaining, "she's been nervous there alone."

"And then she met Mr. Rupert," Dad suggests as he turns down our street.

"Yeah. He's scary to us. He's in the reserves. Walks the neighbourhood in his camouflage uniform."

"But to her, he's a strong man," Mom says.

"The only thing I wasn't sure of is whether Mr. Rupert deliberately pinned the gun theft on Attila or whether he really believed Attila took it because he caught him on the surveillance camera," I add. "But Mrs. Klein solved that bit by confessing about not telling him."

Dad pulls the car into the driveway and shuts the engine. "You don't think he just wanted to blame Attila to get him in more trouble because of the mailbox?"

"At first I did. But he looked pretty surprised to hear Mrs. Klein's confession," I answer.

"You'd think the police would have questioned Mr. Rupert earlier about the gun found in the school," Dad says.

"A mistake?" I suggest. "The desk sergeant didn't tell the constables any details about the missing replica."

"Okay, I want to hear the rest of this. But I really need to hit the bathroom," Mom says as she dashes inside.

We follow her out of the Grape-mobile and into the house. Dad immediately takes the meat loaf from the freezer and sticks it in the microwave.

"Anyhow. All that figuring out is amazing. You don't want to be a detective when you grow up, do you?" He opens the fridge and tosses me a head of lettuce.

I catch it. "No. Just wanted to help a friend."

"Ha! You finally admit you can have a girl as a friend." He pitches me tomatoes, one by one.

"Who's got a girlfriend?" Mom returns from the bathroom. "What else have I missed?"

"Nobody, nothing, Mom. You heard the whole story." Dad throws me an orange pepper, then an onion.

"Rushing for the bathroom reminded me of a tidbit I heard. You know that flight attendant I sometimes see who does the Toronto–New York run?"

"The one who was delayed because the kittens shut down the Manhattan subway?" I rinse the lettuce.

"Yes, that's her. She says John F. Kennedy airport now has a bathroom for pets. Here, give me the vegetables. I can start chopping."

"Really?" I ask. "What's the bathroom like?" I rinse off the tomatoes and hand them and a cutting board to Mom. Then I begin tearing off leaves of lettuce.

"Very nice, apparently. Single-stall with artificial turf and a drain. They've added some cute artsy touches, too, like paw prints on the wall, a little red fire hydrant ..." Mom chops the tomatoes twice as quickly as I can and they're all in even quarters.

"Artsy touches are soul food," I repeat Mrs. Irwin's words. "Everyday art is *sooo* important."

"Yes, that's true. And every airport should have a pet bathroom," Dad says. "Imagine dogs or cats having to hold it or being forced to go in their cage."

"Well, pet bathrooms are the way airports are going. In the U.S., airports serving over 10,000 passengers per year are mandated to get one," Mom says. "I've heard that Frankfurt Main International in Germany serves more than 110 million pets a year in their animal lounge."

"Wow."

"Twenty-five animal keepers and twenty-five vets work there," she says as she chops the pepper. "So what's this about a girlfriend?"

"Nobody has a girlfriend, Mom. Dad's ordered Renée a Noble Dog Walking uniform, so guess I'm going to share my dog-walking money."

"Does she help you?" Mom asks. "Or just keep you company?"

"She's really good with Ping, who's pretty hyperactive."

"You think Ping's hyper? You should try walking the Yorkies!" Dad says. "Renée sure comes from an artistic family."

"Yeah. Renée's pretty interesting, too. Notices just as much as I do. More than Jessie. Forces me to do stuff I don't want to, though."

"Kind of like a wife." Dad grins and Mom punches his shoulder.

I think for a moment about all the stuff that wouldn't have happened to me without Renée's pushiness. Even if I have to walk past more junk on garbage day or constantly defend her scary brother, having her help me is really a brilliant arrangement. "More like a really good friend."

SOME PEOPLE COUNT THEIR BLESSINGS, BUT STEPHEN NOBLE COUNTS HIS MISTAKES.

THE GREAT MISTAKE MYSTERIES

BY SYLVIA MCNICOLL

BOOK 1

IS IT A MISTAKE TO GIVE IN TO DOGNAPPERS?

BOOK 2

ART IS MISSING FROM THE NEIGHBOURHOOD. HELP STEPHEN AND RENÉE CATCH THE CRIMINAL.

BOOK 3

CAN STEPHEN AND RENÉE SOLVE THE CASE OF THE MISSING PYTHON?

THEY'RE DOGGONE GOOD MYSTERIES!